**WHAT ROLE DO CHILDREN PLAY
IN *STAR TREK*?**

**HOW DOES CAPTAIN PICARD
STACK UP AGAINST CAPTAIN KIRK?**

**WHAT WAS SYBOK'S TRAGIC MISTAKE
IN *THE FINAL FRONTIER*?**

**JUST HOW "DIFFERENT"
ARE HUMANS AND VULCAN?**

Here's your chance to gain a whole new perspective on *Star Trek*'s finest, from Kirk, Spock, and McCoy, to Picard, Riker, and Data, as you delve into this brand new collection of facts and fancy about the crews of the *Enterprise*, old and new. From the flaws and fun of the motion pictures, to a fuller study of the truth about *pon farr,* to the ways in which the various episodes and films reflect our own changing society, there is a wealth of trivia and treasures for both long-time fans and newcomers to the excitement and adventure of *Star Trek*. So board your favorite Federation starship for an unforgettable voyage to—

THE BEST OF TREK #16

THE BEST OF
TREK
#16

EDITED BY
WALTER IRWIN & G. B. LOVE

RoC

A ROC BOOK

ROC
Published by the Penguin Group
Penguin Books USA Inc., 375 Hudson Street,
New York, New York 10014, U.S.A.
Penguin Books Ltd, 27 Wrights Lane,
London W8 5TZ, England
Penguin Books Australia Ltd, Ringwood,
Victoria, Australia
Penguin Books Canada Ltd, 2801 John Street,
Markham, Ontario, Canada L3R 1B4
Penguin Books (N.Z.) Ltd, 182-190 Wairau Road,
Auckland 10, New Zealand

Penguin Books Ltd, Registered Offices:
Harmondsworth, Middlesex, England

First published by Roc, an imprint of New American Library,
a division of Penguin Books USA Inc.

First Printing, March, 1991
10 9 8 7 6 5 4 3 2 1

ROC IS A TRADEMARK OF PENGUIN BOOKS USA INC.

Printed in the United States of America

CONTENTS

STAR TREK: THE NEXT GENERATION— REVIEW AND COMMENTARY

by Walter Irwin

Rumors had been flying fast and furious for months: A new Star Trek series was in the works. One source said that it was to feature the adventures of Captain Sulu and First Officer Saavik, with occasional visits from the other series regulars. Another "insider" said that the new series would feature new actors in the roles of Kirk, Spock, etc., but that all of the stories would be about them in their younger days. Still another rumor swore that the series would simply take up where the last film left off . . . with Kirk and crew heading out in NCC-1701-A. Well, we now know what Gene Roddenberry was really planning. But for a Star Trek fan, the bottom line is simple: Is it Star Trek? In the following review, Walter asks the same question, and provides not one but two answers.

Star Trek: The Next Generation made its debut with a two-hour telefilm titled "Journey to Farpoint." The show qualified as a pilot not only in that it was the first episode filmed, but also in the more prosaic sense that it introduced the major characters and their relationships to each other, as well as setting up the world they inhabit and the rules it works under.

As a pilot film, the episode was entirely successful. We met the crew—Captain Jean-Luc Picard; his first officer, Commander William Riker; the second officer, Lieutenant Data; Ship's Surgeon, Doctor Beverly Crusher; Chief Helmsman Lieutenant Geordie LaForge; Security Chief Natasha "Tasha" Yar; and Bridge Officer Worf—and got a nice, if incomplete, look at the new ship, the USS *Enterprise*, NCC-1701-D, and its company of Starfleet personnel and their civilian families and friends. We also met, in true pilot tradition, the being who looks as if he (it? she? they?) will become the recurring nemesis of Picard and company, the enigmatic "Q."

As a story, the film was less successful. The story lines of Q's threat and the mystery of Farpoint were not well integrated. Q's acquiescence to Picard's suggestion that he judge them by their success on Farpoint was too quick, a little too patently for script purposes. Even worse was Q's blatant attempts to force Picard to choose wrongly at the climax of the episode. The last thing needed then was a false infusion of "suspense": we in the audience had already guessed much of the mystery and knew Picard must have, too. The amateurish theatrics which ensued helped to destroy much of the sense of wonder the moment should have generated.

It is a science fiction axiom that the actions of aliens, being of alien motivation and therefore incomprehensible to humans, do not necessarily have to make sense by human standards. Unfortunately, many science fiction writers have seen this as license to create creatures/characters that can do literally anything, without the need for reason or explanation.

Such is the case with Q. We—and Picard—are not given sufficient reason why humans are the targets of his rancor. One would reasonably expect that any race advanced enough to perform seeming miracles would be advanced enough to recognize historical evolutionary progression among humans—or, if nothing else, to read the minds and emotions of the crew of the *Enterprise* and see in them that their intentions are benign. Since this does not happen, we are left with only one conclusion: Either Q (or "the Q") simply do not want to understand humanity, or they cannot—so much for godhood.

We are left, then, with yet another childish, spiteful, petty tin-plated super-alien acting like a complete ass by any reasonable standards of behavior simply for the purposes of the plot.

It's old, it's tiresome, and it's been done before, too many times. In fact, it's been done at least four times on Star Trek alone! It was quite disappointing to see Gene Roddenberry and his staff emerge with such a hackneyed plot device for the first new Star Trek episode.

How much more interesting it would have been to have Q be a calm, reasonable being engaging in civilized debate with Picard. Yes, the threat of destruction would still have been there, and it would have been even more chilling. Who wants to think that he would fail a test of ethics when judged fairly and impartially? Especially if such failure would result in the confinement of your entire race?; a confinement that would, sooner or later, result in the death of that race.

The second plot of the pilot, the mystery of Farpoint Station, was not a lot more original, but it was at least handled more effectively, if only because the *Enterprise* crew members went about solving the mystery in a scientific and methodical fashion that smacked of realism. If they didn't catch on any too soon, well, that happens in real life occasionally. And the proper scientific method is to investigate all possibilities before making a hypothesis.

My only complaint with the Farpoint mystery scenes is the overly histrionic fashion in which Groppler Zorn acted and the offhand manner in which he and everyone else described the methods of "construction." It is hard to believe that the Federation would have decided to build a Starfleet station without knowing *how* it was to be built; simple security and integrity of construction would demand more than a cursory examination, if nothing else. And if Groppler Zorn and his people acted in the same sullen, evasive manner to Starfleet negotiators as they did to Picard and Riker, the real mystery is why Starfleet ever accepted the deal in the first place.

The ending did manage to mesh the two plots effectively enough. The scenes of the alien "jellyfish" creatures reuniting were well done and quite moving. And it did bring back a little of that old Star Trek spine-tingle to hear Picard say, "Let's see what's out there!"

There is no doubt that Patrick Stewart as Captain Jean-Luc Picard is the star of the show. Although not a particularly impressive physical specimen, he has a presence that literally takes command of every scene; the same kind of presence an actual Starfleet starship commander would have.

Stewart's Shakespearean training is evident with every line he speaks. And the viewer has to be careful these days, for Stewart holds to the time-honored British tradition of "throwing away" the occasional line. Let your attention wander, and you just might miss something.

The ship is new to Picard but not brand-new. He is still finding his way about and around her, but does not lack for confidence in either himself or his ship. That he is uncomfortable with children comes as no surprise—the surprise is that he feels it a flaw, and makes sure it is one that is corrected before it hampers the operation of his ship.

This scene, as well as the one in which Picard orders Riker to manually dock the ship, tells us that Picard is a perfectionist, expecting nothing but the best from himself as well as others. But he is not a martinet; he understands the necessity for families aboard the *Enterprise* (although he may not agree with the policy) and works to make the best of what he sees as a bad situation. Picard is the kind of man who tries to plan for every eventuality, and I suspect that if he has any qualms and second thoughts about his command, they come from the things he feels he should have foreseen and did not.

He's not a physical man. We will not see Picard leaping from his command chair to rush down to an unknown planet, nor are we likely to see him in one-on-one combat with an enemy. He is a cerebral captain, given to consideration of a problem before acting, taking all possible available advice, waiting to see rather than waiting for the main chance. Picard may act wrongly, but he will never act impulsively.

The problem with such an approach is twofold: First, Picard probably is not a gambler. Risks are part of the job, but Picard will believe more in preparedness than bluff. Although this is probably a realistic view of what a starship captain would be like, it does tend to downplay the thrills and fun a little bit. We Star Trek fans have been conditioned to want our captains to be a little bit roguish and unpredictable.

Second, a thinking captain is more likely to capitulate than an "action" captain. Not out of cowardice or a conviction that he cannot win, but out of a desire to make the best of a situation. In the pilot, I felt that Picard surrendered a little too quickly to Q. Yes, he was protecting the families in the saucer section, but maybe it would have been better to put up at least the pretense of a fight. If Q had been savvy enough to pick up on the importance of the saucer, he would have made for it instead of the engineering section.

In all, however, Stewart's Picard is a worthy addition to the ranks of starship captains. He manages to combine dignity and authority with just the right touch of idealism and enchantment with space to be believable. The ultimate test is passed: We would not mind shipping out under Captain Picard.

We cannot yet be quite so sure about Jonathan Frakes's Commander William Riker. Frakes got to do very little in the way of real acting in the pilot, and his scenes as Riker, although plentiful once he was introduced, had nothing to particularly impress or endear him to us. The only memorable scene, in fact, was his short idyll in the forested rec room when in search of Data. I hope that plans call for Riker and Data to become friends, as they interacted very well here, and it was during these scenes that Frakes seemed most at ease.

Obviously, Riker will carry the main brunt of whatever action is to be found in this new series (by all reports, there will be less in the way of violent, physical action than in the original series and the films), aided and abetted by "away team" regulars LaForge and Data. As we now have a reflective captain, we can only expect to have a first officer who is more a man of direct action, and who will counsel same when asked.

It is nice to see Riker acting as Picard's first officer— officially issuing commands, serving as his liaison with the crew, taking responsibility for the day-to-day operations of the ship. Again, it is one of those touches of reality so desperately needed in a science fiction series. (Of course, if Riker really did fulfill all the duties of a first officer of a ship of the line, we would hardly see him. He certainly wouldn't be beaming down; he'd be far too busy.)

Although Roddenberry and Paramount publicity have constantly reiterated that "there will be no Big Three" in this series because "everyone is a star," events of the pilot immediately give the lie to what we all knew was patent nonsense anyway. Picard and Riker sit alongside the ship's counselor, Deanna Troi, in an arrangement that brooks no argument about who is in command and who is important. (Actually, given the likely high visibility of Doctor Crusher, we will probably end up with a Big Four on this show—kind of a "Bob and Carol and Ted and Alice" in space.)

Picard and Riker must, of course, be involved in every major decision, and even though the series postulates that Captain Picard will consult his entire staff whenever possible, making for scenes in which all the regulars put their two cents in, when push comes to shove, there will be two or three figures that the show will focus on.

Focus on, not feature. Everyone will be featured before very long—they are all interesting characters, designed to have a vital element of mystery and excitement that entices us to want to know more about them. We will, sooner or later, learn more about Yar and Worf and LaForge. But in no way will they become the stars of the show.

But Data just might. Dismissed before the series began by many fans as "the worst idea about the show," Data looks to be his own man, if you'll pardon the expression. There's certainly nothing new about android characters—the original series had its share, and so did another Roddenberry project which we'll discuss in a moment—but it somehow seems right that this new Star Trek, with its unspoken devotion to IDIC, feature a character, and, more important, an *officer*, who is not only not human but isn't even "alive."

Brent Spiner, the actor portraying Data, is completely engaging, yet still transmits an intelligence and sensitivity that we immediately respond to. A number of fans have remarked on his scenes with the aged Doctor McCoy in the pilot as sure evidence that he is intended to be the Spock of this new series, but I believe otherwise. I think that Roddenberry saw immediately that Data has more in common with McCoy than Spock, and that is why he was chosen to speak with the Admiral. Gene Roddenberry isn't saying, even in private, but no less of an authority than Majel Barrett Roddenberry has her suspicions that Data might just be one of the last of the Questor androids left by advanced aliens to guide and protect mankind, as seen in Roddenberry's aborted TV pilot, *The Questor Tapes*.

Data looks completely different, true, and there is no other evidence to support such a suspicion, but it's kind of nice to think that Star Trek is connected with the world of Questor.

We also got a brief look at how Geordie LaForge's optical visor fits on, and a hint that wearing it causes him constant pain. It is refreshing to see that LaForge's "handicap" is not played as such—either way. His vision is used as a tool when necessary; his lack of sight is not used as a story point.

Many fans do not know that the character of Geordie is based on a real person, George LaForge. George was an avid Star Trek fan who, although quadraplegic, attended many Star Trek conventions in the early 1970s. His unfailing good humor, bright smile, and quick wit caught the eye and earned the friendship of Gene Roddenberry. Sadly, George died in 1975, but the memory of his intelligence and courage lives on, thanks to Gene Roddenberry and Ensign Geordie LaForge.

A number of fans have dismissed the presence of young Wesley Crusher as a sop to teenage boys, but if I were still a teenage boy, it wouldn't be Wesley I'd like, it would be Tasha Yar. I know that when I was thirteen or fourteen, there was nothing I liked better than a good-looking, tough woman. Of course, I'd probably have been scared to death had I met one.

All kidding aside, Roddenberry probably didn't give much thought to that aspect of Tasha Yar. What he wanted to give us was a young, tough security chief, a woman who combined beauty and a certain measure of femininity and vulnerability with determination and sheer grit. We learned that Tasha (short for Natasha) is a native of an Earth colony that somehow went wrong and became what might be best described as a planet-sized ghetto.

(As much as we want to learn more of Tasha's origins, the tale of how her planet slipped into such an awful state and why the Federation did nothing to solve the problems might make for a story that would be just as interesting, if not more so, than hers. To postulate only one question the scenario raises: Do Federation colonies fall under the restrictions of the Prime Directive?)

I have heard fan comment to the effect that Tasha acted too impulsively in the pilot; other comment says she seems scared or nervous when faced with a security challenge. I must agree that Denise Crosby could have handled some aspects of her character a little better (I personally feel the ever intense expression and short, choppy sentences grow a little grating), but, like everyone else, Tasha is still growing both as a character and as a member of a team. The intensity she displays now might just, in the future, form the basis of an episode in which that intenseness—or the lack of it—is pivotal to the survival of the ship and crew.

Talking about Tasha reminds us of Worf. They seem to be part of a mini-team working on the bridge, both involved with weapons and scanners. They are also both of a temperament.

Worf, true to his Klingon heritage, is quite ready to

fight at all times, and has no hesitancy about speaking out. One of the most interesting moments of the pilot was Worf's anger at being ordered away from the ship before a pending battle. He referred to himself as a Klingon of Klingon heritage—and although he has obviously taken a vow to serve under and obey Starfleet rules and regulations (and restraints!), he *thinks* of himself as nothing but a Klingon as well.

We don't yet know Worf's story—scuttlebutt before the series began had it that the Federation and the Klingons were now allies, which is why Worf (and eventually) other Klingons would be seen onboard the *Enterprise*. Other, later rumors state that Worf was rescued from a crashed Klingon ship as an infant and raised in the Federation. His attitude would seem to refute that scenario, but it is possible. Worf was a latecomer to the original cast—although an extremely welcome one—and was therefore not as completely fleshed out as the others.

I'm going to give Deanna Troi short shrift in this review. Mainly because I feel that she, of all the characters, is the one that Roddenberry and his staff will change the most over the next few months, and what she may become might be different enough to dispel any complaints I might have here. Suffice it to say that I very much disliked both the character and her part in the show.

The most background we got on a character in the pilot was that of Dr. Beverly Crusher. Her husband was killed when serving with Picard, a fact that causes continuing tension between them. Beverly is competent, a little bit sassy, and darned good-looking. If there is to be a continuing romance on the show, I would prefer it to be between her and Picard rather than between Riker and Troi. It would be nice to see a starship captain who came "home" every night to relax and maybe just talk things over with a friend and lover.

Wesley Crusher I really don't know about. He seemed like a pretty normal, likable kid, even though of genius level. There's little enough to say about him now. The danger in Wesley lies in allowing him too much screen time. As I stated before, youngsters who watch Star Trek won't be looking for someone to identify with, so there's no need to feature Wesley every week—certainly no need to allow him to become a Will Robinson character who is always right while the bumbling adults are always wrong. Too, there is the danger that Wesley will come across as just a little wimpy. The best way to avoid this is to keep him interacting with other kids his age—both boys and girls, Gene!—and show him growing and learning slowly but surely, as we all did (and do).

There is much to admire about *Star Trek: The Next Generation*. The ship is beautiful; the special effects are wonderful (although the shift to videotape is sometimes a little jarring); the production values, sets, and props first-rate; and the actors all competent, with a few outstanding. Roddenberry and Paramount have promised to keep this level of quality up, and with the great number of stations running the show, and the consequent influx of money to the episode budgets, *The Next Generation* should remain the best-looking show on television.

The eclectic mix of crew did not work totally in the pilot, but such a large cast needs time to shake out and fall into their respective roles. There is enormous potential among these characters—in Picard, Data, Yar, Crusher, and Worf especially—and with care and slow development and nurturing, they should become worthy successors to our beloved original crew.

So the question remains: Is it Star Trek? The answer is a definite Yes. *Star Trek: The Next Generation* is completely true to the principles and ideals of the original series. It is also a logical development of both technology and socio-military attitudes in the Federation, the kind of extension of the Star Trek universe many fans have always imagined. No, it is not "Wagon Train to the Stars"—but it *is* an extension of Gene Roddenberry's dream, a continuation of the things we know and love and cherish about Star Trek and what it stands for.

There's another Yes, however. *The Next Generation* is also the Star Trek of special effects, aliens (and alien monsters, eventually), glitzy weapons and ships, costumes, and weird-looking beings all over the place. Eventually, it will also be the Star Trek of the books and records and comics and toys and coloring books and pajamas and lunch boxes and . . . And conventions. And jokes. Wisecracks. Snide remarks. The typical dual attitudes of "If it's popular, it can't be good" and "I hate Trekkies" that we despise so and have so sadly become accustomed to.

Yes, my friends, *Star Trek: The Next Generation is* real Star Trek. And once again we will have to take the good with the bad. Gene Roddenberry and his wonderful staff, along with Paramount Television, have presented us with a wonderful and—to be honest—woefully overdue gift. But, as always, we are the bottom line: It is up to us to keep the show alive, to make it so much more than even Roddenberry imagines it could be, to make it part of our fandom, our universe, our lives.

When you get right down to it, friends, it doesn't matter if *The Next Generation* is "real Star Trek." It doesn't matter because *we* are the real Star Trek.

WALKING THE DECKS
OF THE REAL
ENTERPRISE!

by Sally Jerome

Basically, I am a quiet, reserved, introverted person. Until someone mentions Star Trek. Then my antenna goes up and starts whirling around. I am always ready to set up a display of my collection somewhere or promote Star Trek any way I can.

This was the display to end all displays. And what came about because of it, I would never have dreamed possible.

WXXV-TV, channel 25, asked me to help them promote the then new *The Next Generation* series by placing one of my displays in their Star Trek Day in the Mall promotion. I was more than happy to do so. The Day was such huge success that the wonderful people at WXXV called Paramount and arranged a private tour of the Star Trek sound stages for me and a party of two. I took my son, Lon, and his friend, Paul Felix.

It was raining when my plane landed. Lon met me at Los Angeles Airport and we drove out to Edwards Air Force Base to pick up Paul. By the time we got back to L.A. to check into the Ambassador, it was a monsoon! As we exited the freeway, we saw cars stalled in deep water in the outer lane. A Highway Patrol car was off the road in a ditch, totally covered with mud. The only thing you could see was its antenna sticking up. When we got settled in our hotel room and turned on the late news, we saw on the TV screen the scene we had just passed, mud-covered patrol car and all. The officer had gotten out of the vehicle in time and wasn't injured. What a way to start our weekend!

It was a dark and stormy night, but the day dawned clear and bright! (I always wanted to say that. Does it sound Hollywood enough?) The morning *was* beautiful as we picked up our pass at Paramount. They give you ten minutes to get your pass at the Pass and I.D. Building just behind the Melrose Avenue gate, or you're off the lot! We drove the car to the parking lot and walked the couple of blocks to the left where the William S. Hart Building is. The only four-story building on the lot, it houses the Star Trek offices. Richard Arnold's office is on the fourth floor; that is where we were heading. There was an elevator at the back of the long hallway, but we walked up, stopping at every floor. That way we got to go by all the rooms and peek into the offices through the open doors.

From the start of our day in Richard Arnold's office, to eating in the Commissary, to the company store, where you can buy souvenirs, to walking the studio streets over to the sound stages, everything was better than we ever could have imagined! It was a special unexpected treat to see all of the Oscars and Emmys displayed in a window showcase outside of the Commissary. We even walked past the old sound stage where *King Kong* was filmed (the original, with Fay Wray).

While we were standing outside the gift shop, Ted Danson walked by with a coffee cup in his hand and a briefcase under his arm. He waved and said, "Hi." It didn't take long to realize that if you saw someone you thought was somebody, they probably were. Meredith Baxter drove by in her neat white car and waved, too. Probably at our guide, Richard Arnold. He's head of public relations for Star Trek. But it's nice to think that she was waving at all of us. I don't think she was doing the seven mph speed limit, either. Stardom has its privileges.

Before we got to the sound stages, we went by the city streets sets from *The Untouchables*. They've been used in some of the Star Trek episodes, too.

The first sound stage we entered was Stage 16. This is the Planet set. It has all the space they need to build any planet surface they might want, and the lighting system to make it any color they choose. There is a huge tank that can be filled with water to create a lake. It can be drained and used for caverns and tunnels, as in "Encounter at Farpoint." The police station for "The Big Goodbye" was set up on this stage. It was painted to make the walls above the railings and woodwork looked soiled, giving them a used appearance. I know they do things like this all the time, but we were impressed. Even Paul said he was impressed, and he's usually noncommittal.

Mr. Arnold went to all the doors of Sound Stage 6, but it was "locked down," so we didn't get to see the *Next Generation* bridge. Mr. Arnold told us that some-one had taken visitors on the set and they had turned all of the electrical systems on and had blown some fuses and wiring. It could have started a fire, taking a great deal of time to rewire and repair. I can't imagine anyone doing anything like that! It's almost sacrilegious.

The first Star Trek sound stage on the lot is Stage 9. It has the permanent sets from the movies on it, and they are used as part of *The Next Generation Enterprise* as well. The bridge is the "battle bridge" for the new series. Dixon Hill's office for "The Big Goodbye" was set up in a corner of the stage that wasn't used as part of the permanent sets.

What can you say about walking the decks of the *real Enterprise*? Except that it makes the hair stand up on the back of your neck! Especially when you enter the sound stage and start down the corridor and you realize that the person walking just ahead of you is Patrick Stewart! Captain Jean-Luc Picard himself! It's all there, too. The corridors, crew quarters, transporter room, bridge, "new and just completed" conference room with its gorgeous 3-D Federation emblem, medical sickbay with the "mahogany" diagnostic table, and next to it, the engine room! That was really something else in a whole tour that was *all* something else to begin with!

The engine room is really fabulous: three stories high with a working elevator. When you stand at the railing in front of the main engine and look down, it's painted to give the illusion that it goes on and on. The main engine reminds me of a very high-tech potbellied stove. I mean that as a compliment, because it seems to be somehow very familiar and something you can relate to, and at the same time "outer-spacy." They still have six of the pedestal chairs left from the original series. Now they're blue. Some of the technicians who are working there worked on the original series. The man who pulled the doors open when they went "whoosh" still does.

Gene Roddenberry came on the set while we were there and asked the sound man (also an original) if there was anything they needed. The sound man told Mr. Roddenberry that they needed a new roof. It had rained a deluge the night before and there were buckets sitting around to catch the drips. I'll bet they got their roof!

A closed set doesn't just mean that you can't get onto it without a pass, it also means that the actors can't leave it in their Star Trek uniforms, either! So they eat on the set. Lunch was brought in by a catering service while we were there and they asked us if we wanted to eat with them, but we had already eaten in the Commissary. We did have a snack, though, and this way we got to do both. I wouldn't have missed a chance to eat in the studio Commissary!

There were boxes of Cheerios on the serving table, too. At the time they had their *Next Generation* promotional stickers inside. One of the extras gave me one of them. One was the new *Enterprise* sticker and I didn't have it yet. I was thrilled to get it. Especially at that time, from that place. I hate to tell you how many boxes of Cheerios I bought, trying to win a little plastic *Enterprise*! I never did. A friend of mine needed a box of cereal and he bought Cheerios so I could have the sticker, and he won a little *Enterprise*! With one box! He gave it to me. Some of the extras are "permanent extras," so they will appear in the background of several of the episodes all year long, giving the series a look of continuity. They work as doubles and stand-ins for the cast as well.

We watched them for a couple of hours setting up the scene and getting the lighting just right. The actors rehearsed the scene twice, then the director called, "Clear the set," and the people who had just wandered in and were standing around, left. There weren't many. We were about the only outsiders around that day and we didn't have to leave. Some of the extras were sitting at a table playing cards to pass the time between scenes.

A bell rang loudly and the director called, "First team," and all the actors filed in to do the scene, right past us! And I brought binoculars with me so I would be able to see them! The director said, "Lights," and they flooded the scene with blinding light. Then "Camera," and a man held up a clapboard to record the number of the scene and the take. Then he said, "Action," and they did the scene. I'll never forget one word of the dialogue. They're all very professional and *very* good.

While the sound man was setting up his recorder, a piece of plastic broke off something inside the machine. I couldn't see from where I was standing exactly what it was. He scrounged up a tube of glue from one of the other technicians and fixed it, put the cover back on, and was ready to do the scene. The reel-to-reel recorder was about the size of my old Beta VCR. It didn't look new, but it did look like it was a very expensive unit. The man operating the microphone boom during the take would swing it so fast from one actor to the other that I was afraid he was going to bop one of them on the head, but of course he never did.

Walking down the corridor of the *Enterprise*, I noticed one of their "alien" potted plants sitting to the left of one of the doorways. It was the one with lavender-colored, saw-toothed-edged leaves. I had seen it in some of the episodes that had already been shown on TV, and it was all so familiar, I felt right at home, but at the same time totally in awe of it all. A roll-about clothes rack with costumes for the cast hanging on it was just outside the conference room. One of the beds from sickbay was in the corridor. They store some of the equipment they're not using in the room of the permanent sets that they don't need for that particular episode or scene. It was a real trip to brush by the clothes rack and even get to touch the plant and those six chairs from the original series!

I was amazed at all the cables and electrical equipment all over the place. It's really dangerous and you could trip over something and have an accident if you didn't watch your step. But all that equipment is what makes our *Enterprise* fly! The one thing that sticks in my mind in this high-tech, special-effects age is that they have to push the camera manually on smooth wooden planks while filming. That really surprised me, although it's nice to know that there are still some things machines can't do.

When it was time to leave, we went out the opposite side of the sound stage from where we'd entered. The door opened up onto a group of trailers for the cast. They had all put their personalized hand-drawn signs on the doors. Gates McFadden was in her trailer waiting to do her next scene. She was dressed in a beautiful pink suit that looked like it was straight out of the 1940s. It was. She said that every time she rehearsed the scene in it and knelt down, it would wrinkle and she'd have to call wardrobe to steam press it, and that was hard on her legs and nylons.

I hadn't really said much all day and I figured I could ask one personal question without getting into too much trouble. Besides, the tour was all but over and there was no way they could take my day away now! So I asked her why she had changed her first name from Cheryl to Gates. Her answer really surprised me! She told me her mother's maiden name was Gates. My mother's maiden name was Gates, too!

She had always wanted to use it as her stage name, and the role in the series gave her that opportunity. Were we both surprised to have the name Gates in common. The time frame of "The Big Goodbye" put her at about my mom's age in the Forties, and she looked so much like her in that pink suit, it was uncanny. As we said our good-byes, she commented on how much she liked the brown leather bomber jackets Lon and Paul were wearing.

Just to the right of the casts' trailers was the makeup trailer. The makeup man was just starting to put Data's makeup on as we walked by.

My day was over. What can you say about a dream (that you never even dared dream about in the first place) come true?

Outstanding?

Doesn't do it justice.

Nothing could!

Thank you, Richard Arnold! Nobody ever taken on a tour enjoyed or appreciated it more than I did.

Postscript

During the time we were walking around the sound stages, I wanted to reach down and pick something up off the floor. A sliver of wood, peeling paint, dust, anything! There probably was nothing there. I didn't look to see. It was just a thought, and I'm surprised it had even crossed my mind. It's just not something I'd do.

While we were on the sets, Mr. Arnold told us to stand back and be very quiet. We did, and we were. When we left, I discovered I had paint all over the back of my jacket! I'll never wash it! I couldn't take the chance of washing out the paint! I got my souvenir!

This is my official thank-you to WXXV-TV 25. I could fill all the paper in the world with thank-you's and it still wouldn't suffice.

We had a wonderful weekend and did some memorable things, but they all pale beside walking the decks of the *real Enterprise*!

CHILDREN IN STAR TREK

by Elizabeth Ann Osborne

As we all know, there were many different themes dealt with in Star Trek. Questions about war, racism, traditional political and social structures, and religion were the ideas of many shows. Many of these themes were part of the growing disquiet of the Sixties, the angry decade. The Sixties was a time of great struggle between the generations. On several Star Trek episodes, either as the main story or as a sideline, the relationship between generations was shown and explored. Rarely were children shown or discussed directly, but in more than a few episodes, issues and ideas about children were shown. I plan to examine these episodes and see what they have in common, what they were trying to say, what they did say, and some explanations for those statements and what they say about the characters.

In all, the portrait of children in Star Trek is a negative one. Star Trek took the more conservative view of children. As an outgrowth of the times, the late Sixties, the series shows a fear of power being held in the hands of children and a belief that they should always be under the control of more adult persons. While the show recognized the need and the desire people have for children, the portrait of children is such that one may wonder why anyone would want them. This is shown very well by Captain Kirk, who often has a struggle dealing with children and, at times, a real dislike of them as well.

Intellectually, Kirk knows that children are important. In "The Apple," Kirk and the landing party meet a society that has no children. It has no need of them since there is no death and everything is maintained by the local god-computer. Kirk announces that this is a sign of a stagnant society and later destroys the computer, bringing children and death into an Eden. Of course, the computer was about to destroy the *Enterprise*, but Kirk makes it clear by telling Chekov and a young yeoman to give the natives lovemaking lessons. Strangely enough, in a similar episode, "This Side of Paradise," Kirk does not make the same judgment. Despite five years and very healthy and happy colonists there appear to be no children around. Kirk does note the fact there is no livestock, but no one notices any lack of children. (Talk about a passive society.) In "The Devil in the Dark," Kirk finds out that the destructive behavior of an alien is a mother trying to protect her children. In "The Wink of an Eye," Kirk understands the Scalosians' desire for children, he just has other plans for himself.

Many Star Trek episodes deal with power and rebellion by children. The first episode to deal with children or young people directly is the very well made "Charlie X." Charlie Evans is brought aboard and begins to cause trouble for the crew. Sweet Charlie is easily embarrassed, and when the crew members start to tease him, he starts to hit back. Charlie goes off the deep end and seeks revenge with his great power until he has to be removed by the elderly appearing Thasians. The dangers of that much power in the hands of a young person is graphically pointed out. For years I could not watch this episode because I felt too much for Charlie Evans and the way I felt about my own teenage years. I felt he was badly treated by Kirk, and most of the crew seemed to enjoy his pain rather than try to be helpful.

The next example is also a look at teenage rebellion. In "Miri," Kirk and the *Enterprise* find a planet where all the adults are dead and society is run by children. A disease kills them when they become adults. Of course, despite the fact that the children have been living that way for three hundred years, the society is a shambles because children are running it. Kirk and the landing party need the help of the children, or at least Miri, so the landing party can find a cure to the disease and return to the ship. Miri falls in love with Kirk, but is crushed when she sees him comfort the adult Yeoman Rand. Kirk later hunts the children down and, although very sick, yells at them that they will all die if they don't cooperate with him. This causes the children, who have been living for three hundred years by themselves, to follow in behind and join forces with Kirk. After getting the children to obey him, Kirk, McCoy, and Spock find a cure and leave the planet with the children in the care of adults. Kirk is sure that the children will enjoy being told what to do, and announces that all children want someone to tell them how to live their lives.

In "The Squire of Gothos," an alien child forms an

imaginary world and captures the *Enterprise*. Kirk battles with him, only to fail. He is saved when the alien's parents come and take him home. It was another episode of the dangers of power when in the hands of a child.

The last episode to deal with children is "And the Children Shall Lead." Often called one of the worst Star Trek episodes, the show deals with a group of children whose parents have committed suicide. Controlled by an evil alien power, the children try for a short time to take over the ship, until Kirk shows them pictures of their families and reminds them how much they loved each other. The crew's relationships to the children are similar to those seen in "Charlie X": Spock is suspicious and hostile; McCoy is friendly and protective; Kirk tries to help but leaves the job of caring for them up to McCoy and Nurse Chapel. Kirk is mainly interested in what happened to the children's parents. He tries the gentle way to get information out of the children and fails. He tries to talk to the eldest, Tommy Starnes, as an adult, but that also fails. The look he gives is of a bachelor who is suddenly forced to deal with a handful of children. Stock comedy situations between the children and Kirk fail to protect his ship, and the children easily take it over by using their powers to influence the crew. Kirk defeats them by exposing their leader as evil and causing the children to reject him and the power he gave them. Again, the danger of power in the hands of children is shown.

Even unborn children can be a problem in Star Trek. In "Friday's Child," an unborn child involves Kirk, Spock, and McCoy in a tribal war. In "The Paradise Syndrome," Kirk's child by Miramanee is a symbol of his new roots on the Amerind planet. Its death is a breaking of those new bonds so he can be free. In fact, the only episode that shows a child in a positive light is "Operation: Annihilate," in which Peter Kirk spends the entire episode unconscious on a bunk in sickbay.

Where Kirk does deal with children well is in the many episodes in which the child is an adult and the parent an older person whom Kirk and the child must defy. Kirk is thus able to deal with the child on an adult level. Often the child is a woman whom Kirk tries to seduce or otherwise gain support from. "The Conscience of the King" and "Miri" are two prime examples of this; "The Mark of Gideon" and "Requiem for Methulesah" are other versions. In "Court Martial," Jamie Finney, the daughter of Ben Finney, at first believes Kirk killed her father, but later comes around to support him. "The Cloud Minders" employs Spock in much the same way.

Many young people support Captain Kirk, especially when he becomes a father figure to them. In "Obsession," Kirk deals with one of his former captains and uses him to end some of his guilt over a past incident. But Kirk also treats the son, Ensign Garrovick, as unfairly as he did himself so many years ago. In "A Piece of the Action," an old-before-his-time street kid with a knife helps Kirk and Spock break into the headquarters of a local gang boss when they promise him he can "watch the hit." Kirk gets in by pretending to be the boy's father.

"The Way to Eden" provides a look at both sides of the way Kirk handles adult children. In this episode, Kirk gets along well with "adult" Chekov, but not with the childlike "space hippies" from the same age group.

The one major adult child-to-parent episode, however, is Spock's—"Journey to Babel." Spock is treated as a wayward child by his father until events allow them, at last, to speak as equals. The two then go a long way toward fixing their broken relationship.

The conflict between generations is shown even in the Star Trek movies. Kirk pushes out a younger Will Decker (the son of Commodore Decker) from the captaincy of the *Enterprise*, believing that no one but he himself can deal with the problem. Decker, however, shows up Kirk by knowing more about the new, redesigned *Enterprise* than the admiral does. Kirk's pride is hurt and he is forced to start treating Decker as an adult rather than a "boy commander."

In the second and third films, Kirk meets his son, now a man possessing very different ideas than Kirk. Their relationship begins with a fight and only later, after much has happened, ends with adult respect on both sides. It is a shock to Kirk that neither Decker nor David need his help in growing up, and Kirk has to respond to David as an adult, not as a small child or an adolescent over whom he has any rights. Late, Kirk is saddened by David's sudden death, but again duty takes hold and Kirk bounces back to his original heroic form. Indeed, in all three films Kirk makes many jokes about the nearly adult cadets, referring to them as "a shipload of children," and in *The Search for Spock* mentions that the *Enterprise* "seems like a house with all the children gone." He seems surprised when they don't need him.

Spock's relationship to children as children is almost

nonexistent. He sees them as future adults and often dangerous, illogical beings. His own strict and unemotional upbringing on Vulcan is probably the cause of this behavior. McCoy, on the other hand, is an emotional man. He also has been married and has a daughter by his ex-wife. Although his marriage broke up, McCoy has had the most experience of the three in dealing with children, explaining why he is the most effective at dealing with them. Kirk is caught between these two poles.

An example is Charlie X. Charlie is treated differently by each of the three. McCoy gets along with Charlie right from the start. Spock treats him with a mixture of indifference and suspicion. Kirk has a more difficult time of it. He wants to be helpful to Charlie, but on an adult level. When Charlie tags him as his father figure, Kirk becomes very uneasy and tries to push the job off onto McCoy. Failing that, he gives Charlie a much embarrassed birds-and-bees speech, and ends up yelling at him (a common way Kirk tries to deal with children).

In "Miri," Kirk gains Miri's help in a surprisingly adult way—he flirts with her, a thirteen-year-old girl. As mentioned, Kirk tries to talk to Tommy Starnes as an adult about what happened on the planet Triacus, but fails there, too.

Kirk holds positive ideas about children, but he finds the actual handling of them hard and unpleasant. He deals better with them as small adults and when that fails, he ends up using anger and threats. However, he often tries to control members of his crew and other young people by playing the role of a father figure.

Kirk's relationships with children are often similar to his relationships with women. He likes them, sees them fulfilling a need, but wants to remain free from emotional ties and responsibilities. His desire to remain free causes him to refuse a role as a real father, despite the evidence that there are quite a few fathers in Starfleet (McCoy, Finney, Matt Decker, Captain Garrovick). Knowing that children are important to a civilization and the emotional need they fulfill, Kirk is pulled in two directions by his inability to deal with them.

In many ways, Star Trek mirrored a belief in the rightness of strong control of children and the necessity for a certain seen-but-not-heard attitude from them. Small children with extraordinary powers and young adults who do not respect and obey the older authority of Captain Kirk and the *Enterprise* are often shown as a source of danger or disruption in Star Trek. It is easy to believe that those who were creating Star Trek were examining the role of youth in the Sixties, and that they feared the new youth culture had produced uncontrollable offspring with dangerous powers. The dangers of placing power in the hands of children was seen in many episodes—how frightening, then, to see the children of the Sixties amassing political power and media influence and, perhaps worst of all, doing so without the guidance of a benevolent, adult "Captain Kirk."

STAR TREK AND
THE MIRACLE MYTH

By Joyce Tullock

Our need for miracles has not changed over the millennia. For this reason, in a day when that which was once miraculous becomes the mundane (flying, cooking a meal in minutes instead of hours, surviving serious injury or disease), we look for other kinds of miracles. Nowadays in our culture we need something big to offer a sort of therapeutic catharsis in a world gone mad. So most especially in our mythology of written and visual escape, we look for the apocalyptic type of overpowering happening that cannot (or at least cannot yet) take place in the real world we know. And it has to be good, because today's miracle is tomorrow's everyday occurrence.

In Star Trek, the miracles most prominent involve this apocalyptic vision of the possible. Well, maybe the just barely possible, once you accept where and when you are when viewing the series, old and new. For the most part, I will refer to the two series simply as Star Trek. They are the same universe at different points in time.

There are different kinds of miracles, of course. Human ones, like McCoy carrying Spock's *katra* and surviving the transference of spirit to spirit. What a beautiful story. A true summation of the Friendship. My personal favorite Star Trek episodes involve this kind of personal, human, deep-from-the-soul story of sacrifice, trust, and love. In such cases we get to see our fellow humans (however alien for the sake of surrealism) at their highest potential.

In Star Trek, we've seen resurrection more times than we can name. What David Gerrold used to call the "almost death" until suddenly it became okay with him when Spock got the ax then came back in *Star Trek III: The Search for Spock*. Now, there's a miracle for you. Nimoy not only got himself resurrected in that film, but he seemed to find his own personal resurrection at that time, coming back to Star Trek at a point when it had appeared he had walked off, hands thrown up in disgust.

Nimoy, you see, had no more appreciation for *Star Trek: The Motion Picture* than most of the cast did. However, he'd been struggling with the Star Trek phenomenon for years, and the first movie's stilted interaction of the characters evidently brought all those feelings to a head. But now we can recognize that *STTMP* wasn't made to be a Star Trek episode (although in the continuing saga it is a *vital* link, showing the growth of the characters since their separation and the emotional damage suffered by the Friendship since the end of the five-year mission; their behavior in *STTMP* was logical, human, natural, and as one would in reality expect it to be, their ultimate reunion part of the miracle). *STTMP* was meant, unlike the episodes that followed, to be a motion picture. It was meant to be science fiction, and had as its director

Robert Wise, father of the timeless *The Day the Earth Stood Still*.

Wise thought he was directing a feature-length film, a science fiction film, and he went by the rules he knew, focusing on typical science fiction melodrama and the awesomeness of Vejur rather than on the kind of heart-stirring character interaction we like in Star Trek (which is, like it or not, a form of soap opera). Boy, the poor guy missed the mark on that one. But in the long run his film works, giving us the connection we need from old series to new movies.

Back to the movie. *STTMP* was and still is the ultimate Star Trek "miracle play," the greatest apocalypse of spirit. A new being—part human, part Deltan, part machine—was born. How I wish we could meet this god child again! What possibilities for Star Trek today! But we become so wrapped up in the miracle of creation in this movie that we forget the even more vital miracle—Earth was saved. No, not just the Earth, the whole darn universe! Now here's something we can really latch onto if we try. Paramount sure did. All the movies revolve around the impending doom of the universe or at least the Federation, and most specifically the Earth. Lucky for us we can always depend on one thing: Jim Kirk's ability to pull off a miracle.

Unlike the Doctors Marcus, who overrated their own abilities, Jim Kirk really *can* cook. The best, most positive, most doggone righteous thing about Star Trek from the very beginning of the series until now, is that people like Jim Kirk exist in it. He is, in an artistic sense at least, a miracle of his own making. He does not quit. He knows what to value and what to leave behind.

Those who mourn the *Enterprise* have not been up in the vast, cold, uncaring loneliness of space. Unlike Kirk, they do not taste the difference between what can be replaced and what cannot. He chose his flesh-and-blood friends over the *Enterprise*. He gave up his most prized possession, his ship, to save Spock. A shrewd bargainer, he knew exactly what he was doing. Jim Kirk has lost perspective a time or two (e.g., *STTMP*)—that's what makes him real and what makes his personal miracles worth their weight in *Enterprise*s. After *Star Trek III: The Search for Spock*, we know absolutely that he has come around, that the Friendship has been tempered to absolute, unbreakable perfection. The three are one—different spirits, different attitudes, different perspectives, moving together as an interlocked, positive force. They go on to *Star Trek IV: The Journey Home* to make a miracle once more, to save Earth, perhaps even the universe again. More than that, they bring back something which was lost, a part of Earth's very intelligent spirit. They provide restoration. And restoration is ultimately the story of all Star Trek in one form or another. The universe goes out of balance, Kirk and friends bring it back. There is nothing more apocalyptic than that.

Balance was an important factor in the religious writing of the Middle Ages. In those days the Passion and all the stories that surround it were the equivalent of "fan writing." Arthurian legends were imbued with Christian themes, most often involving a loss and regaining of spiritual balance. They were loaded with miracles designed to bring the world aright. It was a time when the universe was expected to be ordered to an extent we now know is not the case. Ah, different times, different dreams.

Nowadays we just look for a happy ending. It's just as irrational. Maybe more so. But when we look to the escape of science fiction fantasy, which Star Trek is, we look for those darn happy endings. If they don't give 'em to us (*The Search for Spock*), we strike back. Usually by not giving them as much revenue as they'd like at the box office. That's why Desilu and Paramount gave us people like Kirk. He and his kind carry with them that indomitable spirit of the positive. Jim Kirk, to my recollection, has never quit. Not once. It is to Bill Shatner's credit that if he understands nothing else about Star Trek, he understands that. He knows that Kirk is pure energy. Absolute determination. McCoy can quit, because he is representative of typical human nature. Spock can even quit, because he is a student of the odds and at times has too great a respect for the logic of the situation. Kirk is the miracle man. To hell with logic, to hell with how he personally feels—he's a man who does not accept defeat, even if it seems inevitable. Jim Kirk is determined to work miracles, to bring the world back into balance. That is his job. It's what makes Star Trek the miracle play it is, as we've seen in so many episodes.

Kirk shoulders the responsibility of setting things right (according to his interpretation of right) early on in his career in episodes like "The Apple," "The Return of the Archons," "For the World Is Hollow and I Have Touched the Sky," "This Side of Paradise," "City on the Edge of Forever," all the way back to "The Enemy Within." Most of the time, in fact, the crew of the *Enterprise* is striving to put the universe back into balance, and that often—especially in the more ambitious episodes—requires a miracle.

The difference between the Star Trek miracle plays and those of Medieval times is that in Star Trek it is man, not God, who does the work. Always. So Star Trek, resting as it does within the boundaries of the genre of science fiction fantasy, stands guilty as charged by those critics who claim that science fiction is a modern-day replacement for religion. In this sense it is. We find our miracles now in our entertainment. We accept the impossible as myth, but we still require it and respect it very much. In fact, no story (other than documentary or biographical fact—and sometimes even then) in the media of film or literature succeeds much without the miracle factor. Whether it be a personality change (Scrooge's transformation of character in *A Christmas Carol*, Raymond's brother's growth in *Rain Man*)—the small, believable, even possible transfigurations of spirit—or the more world-altering miraculous changes of films like *2001* or *Star Trek V: The Voyage Home*, by which we may assume the world is at once saved, changed, and balance restored, the miracle factor is at play.

In "City on the Edge of Forever," Kirk performs miracles on two levels. The first is the miracle of sacrifice. He finds an almost supernatural strength within himself which allows him to give up the one person (we can assume to this day) to have been his true love, Edith Keeler. That is the personal miracle of Jim Kirk. On a grander scale he performs an earthly miracle. He saves the world from Nazi domination. In the Sixties, remember, we were still struggling with the memories of World War II. That war had been a trauma of the most horrible dimensions, one not easily overcome, and Star Trek's writers and producers knew the powers of evil it could conjure up in our minds. They recognized that fact so well, actually, that they allowed the ugly demon of Nazism to rise again in "Patterns of Force," in which once more Kirk, Spock and McCoy must set things aright.

How indicative of the times that even Jim Kirk, in "A Private Little War," Star Trek's shy acknowledgment of the Vietnam War (then called "conflict") could not make things right. All he could do in this episode was to even the odds, bringing things back into balance by supplying his friends with weapons appropriate for fighting their Klingon-supported opponents. We leave that planet and episode with a sense of hopelessness, much as we would later leave Vietnam. All we can do is hope that good will win out and, to paraphrase words from another episode, good doesn't prevail unless it is "very, very careful." Other than the fact that Kirk is saved from death by the Mugato bite by a beautiful native woman's home remedy, there is no miracle to this episode. It is just about as nitty-gritty an ending as Star Trek ever gets. The only happiness to this ending is that our heroes get beamed up and out before this society evolves into nuclear warfare.

Pause for thought here. Star Trek's continuation, *The Next Generation*, seems to have a penchant for revisiting old episodes—that is, for rewriting actual scripts as if no one would notice. Why, oh why, if they must borrow, don't they instead go back to some of those places, once in a while, that Kirk's crew left behind. Wouldn't it be more interesting to see how things have shaped up on planet Neural after a hundred years, or to see, for example, how it goes on Yonada—instead of rewriting old plots that weren't all that grand the first time around?

Anyway, perhaps "A Private Little War" shows that nations, like individuals, have trouble facing their most imminent problems. Or perhaps it was just Star Trek's dose of reality.

The most awesome miracles, of course, come in the movies, including the very fine pilot to *The Next Generation* and beyond to *Star Trek IV: The Voyage Home*.

The Voyage Home was the voyage home. Star Trek at its best, almost a distillation of what came before. The complete package (for those who can overlook the missing *Enterprise*). We have Kirk, Spock, McCoy, Scotty, Uhura, Chekov, and Sulu. We have alien beings, alien rites, alien ways, even an alien ship. We have the old interaction of characters, the drama and comedy. We even have Mary Sue in our dedicated, attractive, and shyly adventurous marine biologist who is absolutely-the-only-woman-or-man-in-the-world-past-or-future-universe who is equipped to care for George and Gracie whale. Yes, absolutely everything. We have tongue-in-cheek humor. We even have "The *Enterprise*" ("I read you, Mister Chekov").

This story has its flaws, of course. However, I am one blinded by the light and life of *The Voyage Home*. I believe and predict that it represents the movies at their peak. Not that they couldn't be better. They could, indeed, if Paramount had the courage. It's only that they won't be better. The last time Paramount took a chance with Star Trek, they made *STTMP*.

They made almost all of the fans angry, certainly all of the cast. They went and made themselves a science fiction.

I think it's safe to say they won't do that again.

So those of us who still fancy Star Trek as science fiction must face the fact, pay the price. We (meaning Star Trek) are different. Practically a genre of our own. We are by no means the first space opera. But we are better at it than anyone else. *The Voyage Home* is space opera at its very best; fun, robust, full of the energy and warm-heartedness of Star Trek. It is also a great miracle play. The miracle of change—Spock. The miracle of restoration—George and Gracie. The apocalyptic miracle—the Earth is saved from universal disaster.

The Voyage Home is a balanced film. It is framed around Kirk and his renegade crew. It is the closest to a Medieval quest story Star Trek has ever come. The members of the crew are grouped off and each group sent on a quest. Kirk wins the trust of a fair damsel. Spock finds his soul. All of our characters have great texture, are not afraid, as in past movies, to, for the lack of a better phrase, be themselves. I guess when you have nothing to lose, you relax a little.

In fact, the movie has been criticized for its relaxed mood. Too silly, say some fans. Too much making fun of Star Trek. Hear, hear, are some of us taking ourselves a bit too seriously? Star Trek is neither reality nor high drama. It is space opera, let's go with it. It does laugh at itself a bit. It has reached maturity. It deserves a little bawd and slapstick. Let's hope upcoming films can show such dignity.

So our crew is on a real crusade this time. Greenpeace

would be proud. The irony of Earth's problem this time around (we've had so many threats) is that we are our own undoing. Poetic, yes. Impossible, no. We've messed up a fellow Earthly life form, one we didn't—oops!—know was an intelligent species at the time we killed and cooked the very last one. Now the devil has come to collect his due. Or more appropriately, the piper has come and won't stop playing his song.

It's a long, whining, and lonely song, and only Spock can figure it out quickly enough to save the day. Perhaps his outsider perspective allows him to see more quickly that indeed man is not the only intelligent life form on Earth.

In this miracle play, you see, we learn first and foremost that man's egotistical nature—his hubris—has gotten in the way for what appears to be the last time. The big mama space whale has come by the Earth to say hi to who knows—maybe her children, maybe her friends—maybe what she considers to be the only intelligent life on Earth. And nobody's home? Oh, oh. Keep calling, dear.

And keep dialing she does. In layman's terms, her attempts to contact the now extinct killer whales are having repercussions on Earth which surely spell disaster. Our planet is dying. And she just keeps up her mournful call, trying desperately to reach someone intelligent, without success. Boy, oh boy, when you think about it, this is McCoy's kind of stuff!

Kirk and crew know it's impossible to convince this whale of an alien that they're intelligent, too, so they go about the task of rescuing the unrescuable—a job made to order for James T. Kirk. They make a slingshot trip around the Sun (miracle enough for today's average airlines traveler) and end up in our very own day and age. Suddenly we begin to realize the seriousness of their situation. If we could, we'd pull them out of the 1980s. We know what they're in for: the punk rockers, thick-headed military, and primitive surgeons only serve to remind us of just how big a miracle these guys are trying to pull off. Luckily for them, they can utilize our nuclear-contaminated society to the good. They find (by a coincidence that is miraculous in itself, and a bit much) their whales in two helpless, if huge, friends named George and Gracie—who just happen to need a lift to a safer world.

Call me prejudiced, but I like this story because our heroes actually manage to survive our own time. That is no easy trick. In fact, to see the real dangers they could have faced, we'd need a mini-series: drugs, street violence, chemical contamination. We saw some of the traffic hazards. Future shock is here now, and ours is an age on the brink. We are not only in an era of whale killing, we are working on humankind as well and every other life form in between. As McCoy points out, "It's a wonder the planet survived this century."

Well, the whales didn't, so the crew swipes 'em, after some fun here and there about town, and makes the even more hazardous journey home in their bucket-of-bolts Klingon ship. By the way, what a scene that is when the Klingon Bird of Prey appears above the whaling vessel, like some sea demon protecting its own. Very wondrous, very miraculous in effect. Suddenly we are aware of the birth of a myth.

In this movie we see miracles in many forms. The miracle of change—Spock learns to "feel fine." The miracle of resurrection—Chekov would have died if left in the hands of twentieth-century medicine. The miracle of salvation—Kirk's priorities are finally and totally straightened around—he is a captain again. The miracle of redemption—the whales (which our time yet has the power to save) are restored. The miracle of the apocalypse—the Earth is saved from the destruction brought down by its "own shortsightedness."

There is great, great hope in this film. It is open-minded in the old sense of Star Trek, and displays IDIC, applying it to the here and now on our planet Earth. It restores Star Trek's principle of a positive future most vividly. In the final scene, our crew is served justice in perfect balance. The ending, in which Kirk and crew are rewarded with another *Enterprise*, may seem a real fairy tale. It is certainly a small miracle. But their reward is just, free-spirited, in the openhearted tradition of Arthurian legend, and their thanks comes from the heart of a grateful world. I wonder if today, in our own befuddled century, we would be any less generous to such courtly renegades as Kirk, Spock, and McCoy. After all, Kirk and crew saved the whole darn world, and did it in the course of voluntarily returning to Earth to face judgment.

Miracle—modern miracle, that is—must certainly involve change in the human intellect and spirit. It must certainly be that thing which helps a man or a woman overcome drugs or alcohol. It must be that thing which causes people to build shelters for the homeless. It must be that thing which gives the handicapped the courage to compete in sports or the musician or artist the courage to create for himself, regardless of profit or fad. Miracle today is that power, whether it be generated from the heart of God or man, which says yes in a world of adversity. Miracle is the accomplishment of the impossible to good ends. Individually, it is the thing within which creates a newness in a tired soul. Miracle, in old times and new, is inspiration. Kirk and crew did this as well, inspiring the duty-bound bureaucrats and stellar intellectuals of their own day. They were the rogues, the Don Quixotes, who took on the impossible because it was necessary to accomplish a modern miracle.

Now it comes time for me to harp again on *Star Trek: The Motion Picture*. Please hold the rotten eggs and tomatoes; this unfortunate stepchild of the Star Trek saga must be dealt with, especially if we're going to venture into the miraculous. The first miracle of this film is that it made a lot of money for Paramount. The second miracle is that the fans went and went and went and bought the videos (both versions) and had the courage to ask for more. The third miracle is that they *got* more! I mean, not only—by the odds—should this motion picture not have been made, it should not have been a financial success. Nobody liked it, except maybe eleven or twelve of us. Most fans just took the attitude of making the best of a bad situation. Nobody wants to talk about it anymore. It is an embarrassment. Most fans do not even want to remember it.

This film brings us face-to-face with ourselves. This time out, we Star Trek fans had to put our money where our mouths were concerning our avowed interest in science fiction. In this story Kirk and crew are almost afterthoughts. Hollywood did not yet know what to do with in-depth characters in a science fiction setting. The *Enterprise* is the star of the film—beautiful, gleaming, powerful. Vejur is the main character, with its naive omnipotence and amoral presence of mind. Vejur is the innocent off on a quest for truth. The "almost being" in search of a self. It says it wants to meet the creator, because it does not yet have the maturity to understand that, by and large, birth is an universal accident. It cannot comprehend that its creator might in some way be its lesser. It is not so different from the rest of us.

The surrealistic/sexual/reproductive special effects sequences of *STTMP* are there for a reason. Vejur, for all practical purposes, is a being not yet born or even conceived. It is like the egg, waiting to be fertilized by the humanity of the tiny but potent *Enterprise*. This is made clear from the very beginning of the *Enterprise*'s contact with Vejur as it penetrates Vejur's orifice and travels cosmic, erotic pathways (like fallopian tubes) to the mystic center where the ancient *Voyager* probe waits for arousal/stimulation/impregnation—and Beginning. I am aware that some do not accept the surrealistic sexual motif of the film. Too bad, because, accept it or not, it is there and it is real. Watch closely enough and you'll see that even the symbols for the male and the female are present in the graphics.

STTMP is complex in meaning, delivering story on many levels. Unfortunately, those impatient with its "evident" (but not necessarily actual) lack of characterization, give up on it, and cheat themselves of a science fiction extravaganza of exquisite visual story and challenging philosophical questions. What is worse, they are missing out, not taking part in this miracle of creation. *STTMP* is the story of birth, any birth. It is the celebration of life, humanity, and the evolution of future. It is nothing less than visual poetry, a discussion of the content of the human spirit from the ground up.

The trouble with *STTMP* is that it deals with the most basic miracle of all—the miracle of evolutionary creation. Its question is too big, its answers too nebulous. They have to be. We don't know the answers to the questions it asks. What is human? What is life and how does it happen to be? Who and where is the Creator? Of what does God consist? Is man on the evolutionary road to godhood? What is living soul?

This last question is a rather awkward way of phrasing a question which is popping its head up more and more often in Star Trek: How do we define worth? That is, in the same sense of value to the universe, what beings among us do we prioritize as having those supreme rights to life and happiness we have until this point bequeathed only to man and God?

It is the single most extraordinary and important question of our era. In 1980 *Star Trek: The Motion Picture* asked it over and over again. No one was listening. Then Leonard Nimoy's *The Voyage Home* asked it once more. It got a little more attention. "To hunt a species to extinction," Spock says, "is not logical."

As usual, the most human, most obvious, most correct and insightful observations must come from the mouth of a non-Terran outsider, be it Spock, Vejur, Ilia, Data, or some other innocent from the outer worlds. *Star Trek IV: The Voyage Home* hits on a question that is valid today in our own real-life world. Who is to say that another species on Earth is less worthwhile than our own? Does the ability to create technology and the pollutants that go with it determine whether a species has a living soul? (It would be wise for we arrogant humans to remember that there was a time not so long ago when, for example, the tribesmen of Africa and the Americas were considered subhuman. Native Australians were hunted for sport.)

Why is it, too, that these entities from beyond, like Spock and Data, are so often most appreciative of the real life miracle of the community of Earth (including humanity) and the potentials they offer? Well, just as a prophet is not known in his own land, so mankind is so wrapped up in the struggle, it forgets what the struggle is all about. In *The Voyage Home*, we see that in our drive to conquer the planet, we spoil it. We lack the foresight to see that man *is* the Earth. Earth *is* man. We—all the inhabitants of the planet, animal and vegetable—are one life force, and when the balance is upset, it takes nothing less than the superhuman efforts of a Jim Kirk to restore it. Maybe that's why we value Star Trek so much. We know that already the Earth has what may be unsurmountable environmental/political problems, and we must fantasize about a superhero who will one day come and make it right. Nothing less than the once and future king.

In *STTMP*, Will Decker carried on in the superman tradition of Jim Kirk and took what is, as far as I've noticed, the most adventurous step yet for mankind in the Star Trek universe. He took one step beyond human life, to something else. He performed a miracle, saving Earth, perhaps the universe, and joining in the symbiosis of a new beginning. Vejur: machine, Man, Deltan. All of the logic of Spock and more. All the drive and adventurous spirit of Kirk. All the heart and passion of McCoy—and we can guess, knowing Ilia, much, much more. In *STTMP* we witness a transfiguration. A real miracle of machine evolving with human matter. Our boys have pulled off the Big One, overseeing, even making possible, the birth of a new being. We cannot doubt its intelligence, passion, or spirit. We know it is at least our equal, probably more. The beauty of it is, it needed *us* in order to come into the fullness of its existence and to be able to strive toward its full living potential. We are the miracle.

There is no concrete explanation for what occurs during the transformation. That's pretty much a prerequisite for miracles. We are simply led to believe that somehow Vejur had the capability to bring about this combustion of spirit, flesh, and machine. Or maybe it was the very chemistry of their meeting which started the action. Anyway, for all practical purposes, it must go unexplained. That's the way it is with myth and miracle. That's why Star Trek is science fiction fantasy, not the pure, cold science fiction of a more sophisticated type. Star Trek at best is rough around the edges where science is concerned, sometimes downright crude. That's because no matter who writes the original script, you can bet money those producing and directing and scratching final drafts and rewrites know less about science than the average ninth grader.

Please keep your cards and letters. I mean no disrespect. Facts is facts, and we have only to look at the Genesis Project to vindicate my remarks. I know Star Trek has its science advisers and they do a good job— when they're listened to. But if the guy writing a movie script wants a certain effect, he sometimes has to overlook the probable and use his poetic license to edge toward the impossible. Writers do it, too, let's not sweat it. Besides, the crooked roads are "the roads of genius."

What would we do without the impossible, anyway? Jim Kirk would have no reason to live. Spock would have nothing to fascinate him. McCoy would have nothing to gripe about (no, that's going too far, McCoy can always find something to gripe about). All of our Star Trek cast, from generation to generation, requires the impossible task. They are our brave Don Quixotes. Science fiction, after all, is today's version of the miracle play, and our characters are cast in a setting that is indeed the Age of Miracles. Also, the Spocks and Datas in their midst need the stimulation of the impossible once in a while.

In fact, our fast-becoming-as-popular-as-Spock Mister Data is something of a miracle in himself. He is certainly a blessing to the crew of the *Enterprise*. He is a storyteller's delight as well, full of promise with his innocence of character and mysterious origins. Like Spock, he has a certain purity of character. He is the Galahad in our midst.

Data's charm is his search for self. He desires to be, at once, more human-like and yet retain his own identity. He is quick, endearing, determined. He is a refined machine, a miracle even to the technology of his time. He is our foil; like Spock, he holds up before us the mirror of humankind and helps us to see ourselves. He envies us just enough to show us the wonder of being human. He helps us value ourselves. He is his own character, not an update of Spock. We don't want him to be another version of Spock. We want him to be Data. My hat is off to Brent Spiner. I hope he is prepared. There is only one other character as irreplaceable in the Star Trek mythology: Mr. Spock. I hope that Paramount is prepared as well. They will not be able to let this character go. He is already legend.

Data is, in a way, a continuation of the Vejur premise. He is certainly a derivative of it. We know from Roddenberry's remarks in the long-ago past that his vision of the future involves the human/computer/machine evolution of mankind. Data is another offspring of that future image. Mr. Spiner makes it a very believable one, and his character, Mr. Data, gives us a glimpse of wondrous things to come.

Data gives us more than promise for the technological future. When we see him in the pilot with the crusty old Admiral McCoy, we are reminded of the possibilities for change, both in the material sense (the technology of Data) and in the human sense (McCoy's easy acceptance of this computer entity as a fellow being). To this point, these two are the only characters from the two Star Treks to have met face-to-face on screen. How fitting. How wonderful! Someone was thinking. What a perfect way to pass the torch. It is a moment as touching and valuable to the Star Trek saga as the overview of the *Enterprise* in *STTMP* and the ever so natural passing of Spock's *katra* to McCoy in *Wrath of Khan*. There are scenes we might well have done without (the "remember" scene in *Wrath of Khan* was in fact an afterthought), but which cause a cementing effect within the entirety of the saga. They say something more than they appear to on the surface. From time to time we fall back on them, as one remembers small but powerful moments in one's life. We are glad someone troubled to make them. They stay with us. They are part of the memory of the Star Trek universe.

Data helps us appreciate man as a miracle. To him, *we* are. To us, *he* is. After all, so far no one's been able to figure him out. We enjoy his discovery of life, the way he takes part in it at every opportunity and studies it with unending curiosity and enthusiasm. He must have relished meeting McCoy, the most human of humans. How he would (and perhaps did) enjoy the story of Spock's death and revival, and miracle of Kirk's determination, and the power of McCoy's humanity. Maybe more than the rest of us, he truly understands and appreciates what they accomplished.

In *Star Trek IV: The Voyage Home*, we of course learn at last what we should have known all along, if it weren't for our human chauvinism. Man is not the only intelligent being on Earth. Kirk and crew perform their own miracle and restore balance in a distorted universe. Perhaps the acceptance of the rights of the whales George and Gracie helps to establish a precedent for maintaining the freedom of the likes of a certain mechanical being yet to be born (okay, assembled). A thanks to Kirk and crew on behalf of Mr. Data.

Our mechanical friend would have no less fascination for the historical reports of the machine that came to be alive. Mr. Data would tell you that, like the transferral of Spock's *katra*, the Vejur transfiguration falls in the realm of the truly inexplicable. We can't pretend to know how it really came about, we can't even speculate. We know these incidents have something to do with a power we do not understand, and that they are evidence of the unprovable.

Star Trek's miracles, like all miracles, are events of the spirit, human and otherwise. These overpowering moments of transfiguration, salvation, and restoration remind us that ours is a vast universe, that omnipotence is a mathematical probability in a time and place where all things really are possible. They are miraculous occurrences brought about by man, God, or the laws of space and time. We don't know their cause, but we welcome the mystery.

THE FINAL FRONTIER
IS THE HUMAN HEART

by Mark Alfred

As promised by director William Shatner at the commencement of filming, *Star Trek V: The Final Frontier* is indeed an action film. It includes all sorts of physical confrontation—from falling off a mountain to hand-to-hand combat to horse rustling to shooting photon torpedoes at a god.

But, more interestingly, the movie also examines the souls of the Star Trek family. More so than the earlier films, the turnings of this plot revolve on deeply held beliefs and commitments of characters both familiar and new.

The movie also contains a large amount of bantering and joking, mainly among the Three (Kirk, Spock, and McCoy), but also among the other characters, and this is as it should be. The Star Trek crew has been through so many trials that they are indeed united by their adventures into a family relationship. The embarrassed silence of Chekov and Sulu when admitting to Uhura they are lost is like those of reunited family members reminiscing over long-past arguments or mistakes.

This warm, teasing tone, so similar to the sort of

ribbing exchanged by loving yet rival siblings, is entirely in order here. For what else are these Star Trek movies but family reunions?

As I mentioned earlier, the story line of *The Final Frontier* is generated by the hopes and dreams, promises and fears of the characters. But for the most part, this doesn't mean much impulsive, reckless dashing about as displayed by Luke Skywalker in *The Empire Strikes Back*, when he foolishly zooms off to Cloud City to rescue his friends. The rashness of such behavior shows the contrasting wisdom of the Vulcan abhorrence of spontaneous emotion.

No, the actions of the principals in *Star Trek V: The Final Frontier* came instead from their deeply held beliefs. The characters aren't puppets of a scriptwriter; the story progresses because of who these people are.

We're given an early indication of the supremacy of the heart's concerns in the scene around the Yosemite campfire. Jokes about explosive beans and "marsh melons" aside, McCoy's question, "Why do we stick together in play as well as work?" has only one answer, as I suggested earlier. The Three are one—one family, or, perhaps, like parents or elders to the larger family, the Seven.

McCoy is no longer afraid to say that his concern for Kirk is more personal than medical. Kirk, for his part, may not really be sure why he risked death on El Capitan. I think part of his motivation was the denial of age. Still, he admits his secret premonition, that death will come while he is separated from his friends.

Spock, typically, is less forthright with his confidences. Yet his frame of mind is clear to Kirk and McCoy, as well as to us, who know him so well.

Behind the taciturn mouth and deadpan stare, Spock is enjoying himself hugely. As Leonard Nimoy says in Lisabeth Shatner's *Captain's Log: William Shatner's Personal Account of the Making of* Star Trek V: The Final Frontier, Spock likes to "pretend as if the character is outside the mainstream of the emotional experience, though he really is in touch with it and understands it all." Now Spock "has that little bit of twinkle" to him (p. 174). It's no accident that so many of his statements are like straight lines for his friends. "Gravity of the situation," indeed.

And, certainly, "Row Your Boat" couldn't be alien (oops!) to his experience, given his penchant for diving into a topic—in this case, researching camping out. Today, as probably in the twenty-third century, the song is used in music texts as an example of a round canon. If Spock can recognize and translate the music-based language of the Fabrini, you can bet your ears he would instantly recognize "Row Your Boat."

No, in his humor Spock is showing here what he later says so plainly in the *Enterprise*'s forward observation room: He has found himself. These men are his soul mates. Part of the celebration of their friendship is this ritual of teasing, this game of verbal tennis in which points are earned by letting your opponent score.

Madman or no, Sybok, son of Sarek, came up with a flawlessly logical plan to get to Sha Ka Ree from Nimbus III. We're not told how he came to be stranded here, or why he alone received "the vision." Shatner says, "The off-screen thought is, in the same way a searchlight reaches out, he had gotten too close to the Great Barrier during his travels and the alien placed the thought in his mind" (*Captain's Log*, p. 62). Given Sybok's preoccupation with searching for the legendary paradise Vulcans call Sha Ka Ree, he developed the feeling that it could be found on the planet within the Barrier. I think it is certain that Sybok's heartfelt longings colored the vision he received. Sybok should have considered the words of Terran playwright George Bernard Shaw: "There are two tragedies in life. One is not to get your heart's desire. The other is to get it."

How did Sybok influence his followers to such absolute devotion? Surely he used advanced Vulcan mind-meld techniques to see into the heart of a potential convert. Such complete telepathic and emphatic communion would convince the person that Sybok deeply knew and cared for him or her. The intensity of the Vulcan's feeling, the focused strength of his vision, would also come across in the meld.

Think of it! Somebody knows your deepest pain, your most shameful memories, and still affirms you; he still wants you and needs you. For most of us, I believe, the catharsis of that "sharing of pain" combined with the absolute conviction of Sybok's belief would have us goose-stepping in line, too.

Any popular movement is likely to attract to its skirts those who are not as devout, but merely discontented with the status quo. Sybok probably didn't take the time to meld with (or hypnotize or establish control over, take your pick) the hundreds of followers with whom he overruns Paradise City. His charismatic, single-minded presence is enough to motivate those poor souls, so ripe to answer the call of rebellion against the planetary government and to find a way off "this barren lump of rock."

Nimbus III, in its inception twenty years earlier, was surely a worthy dream, a "planet of galactic peace," administered benevolently by a triad of representatives: one each from the United Federation of Planets, the Klingon Empire, and the Romulan Empire. One wonders, though, if perhaps Nimbus III was established by the rulers of the three governments to get those nagging peaceniks off their backs.

The full text of the scene introducing Caithlin Dar, St. John Talbot, General Korrd, and Nimbus III's origin is given on pages 150-53 of *Captain's Log*. Much never made it into the final print. From it the following is learned:

Soon after the beginning of the experiment, the planet was hit by "the great drought." The settlers began fighting each other, instead of the land, for survival. Of the three representatives, only the newest, Caithlin Dar, feels there's still hope for Nimbus. It's too bad that her hopes are swallowed up by Sybok's *hejira*.

Klingon Captain Klaa is also chiefly concerned with fulfilling a lifelong dream—a dream of blood and destruction, not of peace and goodwill. In these relatively peaceful days—Klaa was a youngster when the Organian Peace was imposed—this Klingon yearns to prove himself a great warrior. He preempts the role of ship's gunner as well as captain, and his crew yields to his will, finding targets for him to practice upon. When notified of the hostage situation on Nimbus III, his first reaction is hope of realizing his dream: engaging a Federation starship. Later, realizing the ship is Kirk's *Enterprise*, Klaa's obsession leaps any intelligent restraint. He resolves to take his little ship against a

Federation heavy cruiser that outguns him ten to one. He knows in his heart that he is fated to meet Kirk in battle and prove himself the greatest warrior in the galaxy.

What is the official status of Klaa and his ship? The *Okrona*, as named in J. M. Dillard's novelization, is probably under official orders to simply patrol the Klingon side of the Neutral Zone—a border patrol. Between the lines of his commission, Klaa accurately divines that he is authorized to do whatever he can get away with. Klingon High Command probably follows the old doctrine of plausible deniability, so familiar even to twentieth-century Terrans. But I think Klaa oversteps even this unspoken boundary; though the Empire wishes vengeance on Kirk for the incidents in *Star Trek III: The Search for Spock*, "the planet of galactic peace" is not the most appropriate place for a showdown!

Down on Nimbus III, the ambassadors are guided by Sybok into confronting their personal failures and pains. Succumbing to his Vulcan mental powers and personal charisma, they join the Galactic Army of Light, a name probably concocted on the spot by gung-ho Dar.

Having worked on maintenance and repairs all the way, *Enterprise* and her crew arrive at Nimbus. The transporter has been busted since departure from Earth, and so the operation to rescue the hostages is commenced in the *Galileo*, a new descendant of the old-model shuttlecraft.

After an exciting battle between *Enterprise*'s people and the occupier of Paradise City, featuring Spock neck-pinching an opponent's horse out from under him, Kirk finds the ambassadors safe within the saloon. But—to his horror—the prisoners he came to rescue instead capture him.

This entrapment is one of a recurring series of betrayals and turnabouts throughout the film. Perhaps the first such surprise is played on the audience, when Scott's log informs us that the beautiful new *Enterprise* we saw soaring into action at the conclusion of *Star Trek IV: The Voyage Home* was in fact an incomplete shell whose most basic functions *gang aft agley*.

Most of the time, as here on Nimbus, the "betrayer" (Talbot) has not become an enemy. Rather, he has a deeper or stronger allegiance that the letdown party (Kirk) didn't know about.

In this first example, Kirk couldn't know that Korrd, Talbot, and Dar have become Sybok's followers. However, in the hostage tape, Dar stated they had willingly surrendered to a leader in whose sincerity they believed. Any hopes that his could be a temporary state of Stockholm (sympathetic hostage) syndrome are soon dashed by the realization that the Ambassadors have been entrusted with weapons.

A far greater apparent betrayal confronts Kirk in the *Enterprise*'s shuttle bay after *Galileo*'s belly-flop landing. Spock's refusal to defend his ship from Sybok is incomprehensible and stunning to Kirk and us. Spock, who gave his very life to save the *Enterprise* from Khan, now just stands there doing nothing.

Thinking Spock is won over completely, Sybok invites the other Vulcan to join him. We're expecting Spock to go along. We figure he'll work his way into Sybok's counsels until it's time to strike back and save the ship. But no. Having let Kirk and McCoy down, Spock then resolves to go into captivity with them.

It's my belief that right here, when forced to give an answer to Sybok's explicit invitation, Spock resolves his conflicting allegiances.

Recall Sybok's attitude toward Spock down on Nimbus III. Like an older brother taking the younger's measure, he congratulates Spock. When he says, "You've caught up with me," Sybok isn't referring to a location, but to a level of consciousness, a goal of attainment, as if welcoming Spock to a real tackle football game with the big kids.

Then, in the hangar bay, under Spock's gun, Sybok just as confidently assumes his kid brother won't take the dare. With a big brother's half-mocking smirk, he challenges Spock to pull the trigger. He "knows" Spock won't do it.

I don't think that is a safe assumption. Spock is not cowed by Sybok's charisma or priority of fraternal place. I believe that Spock is instead simply paralyzed for a moment of indecision—it happens to the best of us. Then the moment is over, and the time for action is lost.

Now, as he's being invited again to join Sybok, Spock realizes the truth of things. Sybok thinks he knows Spock, and presumes too much on that knowledge. Yes, Sybok's relation to Spock would always be tinged with a little patronizing condescension, a generous inclusion of the tardy prodigal brother. Sybok doesn't want Spock the person. He just wants to remove an obstacle from his path to Sha Ka Ree.

Spock weighs this smug offer against his vow to Starfleet and, more important, his spoken and silent pledges to his shipmates. "I have been, and ever shall be, your friend." "The male is accompanied by his closest friends. I also request McCoy." "They are my friends."

In stark contrast to Sybok's self-centered vision of power and personal paradise, Kirk and McCoy know Spock with the discernment of decades of companionship. They value his soul because of (and sometimes in spite of) that knowledge. They treasure him not because of what they want from him, but for who he is, and for who they are with him.

Nimoy put Spock's thoughts regarding Sybok's offer this way: "Although you're my brother, I've gone through more brotherly experiences with these people. I have spent more time with these people. I have been helped, given back my life, by these people. Things that never happened between Sybok and Spock. Therefore, although in blood and name we have a relationship, the relationship with Kirk and the rest in a way is more real, more valid" (*Captain's Log*, p. 177).

For Spock—now that the decision has been made—the distinction is clear. The only way to follow through now is to go to the brig with his hurt and uncomprehending friends.

McCoy is only now coming out of the *Galileo* and doesn't understand what just happened, but in the brig it all comes clear, along with Spock's previously unspoken motivations.

Stoic that he is, Spock unflinchingly yet apologetically admits the essence of the situation: Not only did he betray the crew, but "worse, I have betrayed you." This statement makes it plain that Spock's decision has been made once and for all. His loyalty belongs to those who have earned it. From henceforth Spock wholeheartedly supports "my captain and my friend."

Kirk and McCoy undergo their own revelation now, learning of Sybok's kinship to Spock. This knowledge deflates Kirk's anger and he must admit that his first officer had a valid reason for that fateful second of indecision.

While his commanding officers stew in the brig, Montgomery Scott has his own pressing business. His ship, his bairns, his raison d'etre, is being threatened by an interloping pack of heathens. He must defend *Enterprise*, the child of his heart, from those who would misuse her. So he enlists help in rescuing "his" ship. After springing Kirk, Spock, and McCoy and sending them off to the forward observation room to call for help, Scott heads back to work on the transporter circuits, only to be united with his ship unexpectedly soon.

Kirk feels a similar drive to action. He must rescue the ship from the madness of Sybok's revealed plan. His crew depends on his guidance for their lives—while this crazed, laughing Vulcan intends to take them all across the 9200 parsecs (according to *Star Trek Maps*) separating Federation Space from the galaxy's Shapley Center and go within.

Kirk receives the false Klingon acknowledgment of his distress call as Sybok finds them. Now it is time for us to see what it is the renegade really does to his converts. His mental powers are such that nearby observers also experience the regressed experience.

To Leonard McCoy, son of David, what was at first dismissed as brainwashing quickly takes on a deeper presence. He is subsumed in the spurious reality of his father's dying moment. The horrible irony is apparent: the miracle-producing medicine man couldn't heal his own father. He couldn't even stop the old man's pain.

(Dillard's novelization calls David McCoy's illness pyrrhoneuritis, a rare disease "from the colony worlds" that destroys the nerves of the body and knows no treatment or cure.)

Reliving the moment, McCoy yields to his father's plea and shuts off the life-support bed to preserve his dignity. Then the worst truth is recalled: not long after, a cure was discovered. Leonard McCoy is consumed with the racking guilt that he betrayed his father by giving him what he wanted—the peace of death.

This vivid confrontation with the past enables McCoy to see that no one could have known a cure was on the horizon. His action was the last gift a loving son could bestow on a father.

Spock's sequence is no less traumatic—his birth and implied rejection by his father. Sybok feels Sarek's words "so human" are a dramatic rebuff to Spock's lifelong following of the Vulcan way. He doesn't know of the spiritual growth Spock has since undergone.

A continuation of Spock's sequence was filmed but cut from the final release print. As described in *Captain's Log*, the scene was a reenactment of Sybok's departure from Vulcan.

"Spock, ashamed and self-conscious of his half-breed status, longed to accompany his renegade brother on his journey to find Sha Ka Ree. But Sybok is banished because of his heretical beliefs, and refuses to take Spock with him since Spock, in his need to be accepted by his father as a true Vulcan, has chosen the logical path of his Vulcan upbringing. When the two brothers are reunited, Sybok is able to conjure up Spock's painful memories . . ." (p. 67). But, as we see, Spock has now resolved that pain without Sybok's help.

It's a thrill to hear him put into words what we've observed over the years. In *Star Trek: The Motion Picture*, Spock acknowledged that what he had been searching for was among his friends on the *Enterprise*. In *Star Trek II: The Wrath of Khan*, he was able to openly banter with his friends and freely say that his dying sacrifice was made for friendship's sake. At the end of *Search for Spock*, that friendship with Kirk bridged the gap from memory to comprehension. In *The Voyage Home*, we saw Spock continue that process of growth and integration until, in Nimoy's words, "Spock is able to say to his father, with a twinkle in his eye, 'Tell Mother I feel fine.' It's an inside joke that even his father doesn't get, so Spock has lost his fear of his father. He's grown up. He's a totally grown-up, individual person" (*Captain's Log*, p. 177).

Now, from Spock's own lips, we hear, "You are my brother, but you do not know me. I am not the outcast boy you left behind. Since that time I have found myself. My life is here, aboard the *Enterprise*."

It's meaningful that logic is not what prompts Spock's decision to remain with Kirk. No, he follows his heart.

Before Sybok leaves them, he for the first time completely reveals his obsession. He "knows" Sha Ka Ree's location because he's had a vision from God. Now, this should set alarm bells jangling in the minds of all of us students of "Vulcan mysticism."

As we all should know, Vulcans have a seventh

sense, "the sense of oneness with the All . . . what some humans might call God. Vulcans do not, however, see this as a belief, either religious or philosophical. They treat it as a simple fact which they insist is no more unusual or difficult to understand than the ability to hear or see" (Roddenberry, *STTMP* novelization, p. 86). In other words, at all times Vulcans are sensing the mind of the Creator. But this is a far cry from Sybok's revelation. That he reacts in a way contrary to his own experimental knowledge is a strong hint that whatever is influencing him is certainly not the One. Instead, as we see, Sybok has been promised his heart's desire by a being whose true intentions are only later revealed.

Exactly how the *Enterprise* passes safely through the intense radiation of the Shapley Center to the planet within, when no other ship or probe has been successful, isn't clear, although it should be. (Dillard explains it this way: As a brilliant scientist, Sybok has analyzed the radiations of the Barrier and is able to adjust *Enterprise*'s shields to compensate. Captain Klaa's technicians duplicate the modifications by analyzing *Enterprise*'s shield emissions, enabling *Okrona* to follow.)

Once *Enterprise* is safely past the Barrier, Sybok releases the Three and they come up to the bridge, while Scott resumes working on those darn ol' transporter circuits.

With *Enterprise* in orbit around the Barrier Planet and Sybok and the Three descending in shuttle *Copernicus*, the stage is now set for the culmination of the two emotional currents of the film. This is the horrible irony: The fulfillment of Sybok's grand dream, his heart's desire, is revealed as the ultimate betrayal of that dream.

Sybok, in seeking God in a certain place to the exclusion of every other, has made a grave error in logic. By necessity, the Creator and Sustainer of All must not be localized in one vicinity. The All, the Nome, must be omnipresent throughout creation, and therefore accessible no matter where you are.

To his credit, Sybok does finally realize the deadly error his path has led him to. His sacrifice, I think, is still partly motivated by selfishness. Of course he hopes to buy time for Kirk, McCoy, and his brother Spock to escape, but there's more to it. I think Sybok is, to put it flippantly, so embarrassed he could just die.

Look at what he's done to get here. He overthrew a planetary government, jeopardized Federation-Romulan-Klingon relations, conspired and commandeered a starship, endangered the lives of hundreds of people—and for what? Now, confronted by the taunting image of his own vanity, he realizes how blind to the truth he's been. No, the end does not justify the means. No, shedding blood will not guarantee peace. No, single-mindedness does not ensure truth. Sybok's dash forward to embrace the deceiver in battle fulfills several purposes. It gives his companions a chance to get away. It lets him vent his rage and shame at being deluded. Also important, he is showing the others that he understands how wrong he was.

But a fourth and no less important reason is less obvious: Sybok has devoted his life to this quest only to see it collapse in ashes. He's got nothing left to live for! His final heroic action ties up the loose ends of his failed life in a noble conclusion.

Still, Kirk and company must escape the rampaging being, now doubly dangerous after having been thwarted. Its plan to escape imprisonment had been going so well, until these miserable little insects changed their minds at the last minute.

Thanks to the transporter (finally) being repaired, Spock and McCoy are evacuated to safety. Now Kirk is left alone—alone to die, he's sure of it, just as in his premonition. To exchange one danger for another—the energy creature for Klaa's Bird of Prey—merely prolongs the anguish.

And then comes the Vulcan ex machina. At Spock's urging, Korrd has pulled rank on the hotheaded Klaa and Kirk has been recalled to life.

As originally filmed, Kirk simply arrived on *Okrona*'s bridge, saw Spock and Korrd there, and somehow put things together. However, as told in *Captain's Log*, preview audiences "did not understand why Korrd rescued Kirk." So a voice-over was added, and a new sequence inserted into the scene, "where Kirk confronts Korrd, Korrd exerts his supreme authority over Klaa, and Klaa apologies for his unauthorized actions" (p. 223). I told you so—plausible deniability!

Spock's statement "You were never alone" brings us full circle to the theme of companionship that opened the film. Sybok's manipulations in the teaser are revealed as hollow; true friendship and understanding are reaffirmed.

The final scenes, the reception in the observation room and the campfire in Yosemite, are reiterations of that theme, the value of companionship. Looking out at the stars, Kirk says, "I lost a brother once. But I was lucky—I got him back." Maybe Kirk is familiar with Proverbs 17:17: "A friend loveth at all times, and a brother is born for adversity."

Yes, the crew of the *Enterprise* is indeed a warm and loving family. Not by blood or marriage, but by the most valuable criterion of all—by choice.

Recall again the flashback scene in the observation room. Sybok said to Kirk, "This is who they are. Didn't you know that?"

But Sybok was wrong. We're not the substance of our losses, our regrets, our secret pain. Only small, ingrown souls nurse grudges and define themselves by their shortcomings. No, brave hearts continue to reach out despite sorrow and despair to grow strong, joining other heroic spirits and finding friendship.

And that's the kind of adventure, a journey into the final frontier of the human heart, that we, too, can undertake. So, come on—let's go!

FALLING OUT
OF STANDARD ORBIT

by David Winfrey

Through the use of which type of engines can a Federation starship exceed the speed of light?

How does the transporter work?

What is the top speed of a shuttlecraft?

If you answered "warp drive," "by the conversion of matter to energy, then back to matter again," and "just under the speed of light," you are among the majority of Star Trek fans who take at face value what the series says about its technology—while overlooking what the show's use of that technology demonstrates. Each of the three major incarnations of Star Trek—original series, motion pictures, and *The Next Generation*—have proven both warp and impulse engines capable of hyperlight speeds, shown a transporter based on the space warp and not on the *matter/energy scrambler* principle, and demonstrated the use of warp-powered shuttlecraft. This is not, of course, the conventional wisdom. Generations of fans, as well as artists, writers, film and television producers, have overlooked such facts in their otherwise painstaking recreations of the original Star Trek. But "series reality" speaks for itself.

The following was arrived at by the scientific method. Over a period of years, the behavior of each of Star Trek's "gadgets" was observed, a theory of its operation developed, and the theory applied over the entire course of the series to see if it checked out. If all details of a machine's operation were not accounted for, it was back to the drawing board. (In several cases, a half-dozen or more theories were advanced and discarded.) Finally, a consistent and logical set of starship operations developed. The *Enterprise* thus revealed differs considerably from that generally held to exist—but nothing except the series' own facts and a layman's knowledge of science has gone into its divising. So as is possible, then, this is the "real" technological milieu of Star Trek.

Let us begin with *standard orbit*, a thing the original *Enterprise* always seemed on the verge of falling out of. Whenever power was lost ("Mudd's Women") or diverted ("Return of the Archons"), reentry was but hours away. This little resembles a contemporary space shuttle's orbit, or any position a sane captain would place his ship into; to be prone to decay in a matter of hours, an orbit's perigee would have to actually touch the atmosphere, thus requiring regular application of thrust to avoid burn-up. The logic of such an orbit is elusive.

Say, however, that standard orbit is not in fact an orbit at all, but is instead a state of powered suspension —an impulse-driven hover. Such a maneuver would require tremendous energy, but we have seen impulse thrust take the *Enterprise* to half light speed ("warp point five") in a matter of an hour or less (perhaps far less; transit time to Jupiter is cited in *Star Trek: The*

Motion Picture's first log entry is an hour more than that required at half cee—but Earth appears to recede at about that rate on the viewer almost from the instant of thrust). Compared to such explosive acceleration, to hover is easy. We have seen the *Enterprise* do it: in "Tomorrow Is Yesterday," she was said to be "directly above the Omaha installation and holding there." In this case, of course, the ship was in the atmosphere, with no other choice but destruction. Why place a ship in powered suspension when an actual orbit would be both easier and safer?

The answer lies in an unremarked but implicit aspect of transporter operation. We have seen landing parties beam from one point on a planet's surface to another ("Assignment: Earth," "Angel One"), but we have never seen "shore" personnel using a ground-based transporter network to travel. (The crew did this in *The Voyage Home*, using the Bird of Prey, but only over short distances and at a relatively high power drain. Once the dilithium was well into decay, Scott had "barely" enough power to transport.) When Admiral Kirk arrived at Starfleet Headquarters in *STTMP*, he came not by transporter, but by air tram. We cannot be sure that this was the last leg of the protracted journey described in Gene Roddenberry's novelization, but we can assume that could Kirk have arrived instantaneously, he would have done so. That he did not suggests that he could not—suggests that point-to-point overland transport may be, for all practical purposes, impossible.

To discover why, we need only consider a couple of examples in series dialogue. In "Mudd's Women," Kirk tells the miners he will beam them up on the first pass over their camp. In "The Savage Curtain," Scott reports that "Abraham Lincoln" can be beamed aboard only after Chekov has announced "one minute to overhead position." In both cases, the implication is that ship-to-surface transport must be nearly vertical—that a vessel must be almost directly overhead of the beam site (or within a thousand miles of the zenith, to be precise—a radius cited by Kirk in "Spectre of the Gun" and demonstrated by the New York-to-Cape Kennedy transfer of "Assignment: Earth").

This explains the bizarre practice of standard orbit. Many beam sites would not, after all, be within a thousand miles of a planet's equator, rendering an actual geostationary orbit useless. Only a powered geostationary suspension would allow constant transporter contact. An actual, unpowered orbit would be used only when no beam down was anticipated, as in the case of the initially inhospitable planet in "The Savage Curtain." (Thus the reference to motion toward an overhead position, "synchronous orbit" being established only later; first pass in "Mudd's Women" may imply a real, albeit low, orbit being resorted to in the ship's low-power state.) The apparent interaction of the transporter beam with a planet's gravity makes point-to-point ground transport impractical—a matter/antimatter power plant, such as that in the Bird of Prey, being necessary even at minimal intervals.

Turning now to transport of another sort, let us consider the behavior of Star Trek's "impulse" engines. The term *impulse rockets* dates to the first pilot, "The Cage," from which it was removed at the suggestion of technical consultant Harvey Lynn, who pointed out that "in a sense, all rockets are impulse rockets."

This resulted in Spock's rather comic "Switch to rockets, we're blasting out." By "Where No Man Has Gone Before," however, the term was back—and as early as that episode, it was incontrovertably proven that impulse was a hyperlight-capable system. The *Valiant*, after all, not only reached the galaxy's edge, but bore the title Galactic Survey Cruiser—a role it could hardly have performed were its old impulse engines sublight only.

In *Wrath of Khan*, an *Enterprise* hours distant from Regula at warp five finished the trip on impulse in similar time (less time than necessary to induce rigor mortis in Khan's Spacelab victims), just as she had, years before, stayed safely ahead of an obviously hyperlight doomsday machine, even with her warp drive knocked out.

Impulse, then, is capable of hyperlight—a fact further demonstrated by the arrival of the new *Enterprise*'s saucer section at Farpoint Station under its own power. The saucer takes longer to arrive than the so-called "stardrive section," and we have no indication separation was effected within light *hours* of Farpoint Station.

Starship separation is, therefore, just that: the separation of one ship into two autonomous, star-traveling sections. This aspect of *The Next Generation Enterprise* design is no accident, nor is it new; it recalls instead the similar saucer-and-cylinders layout of the old *Bonaventure*, which Scott described as "the first ship to have warp drive installed" ("The Time Trap"). Knowing that impulse, as well as warp engines are capable of warp (hyperlight) speeds explains Scott's odd choice of words; clearly *Bonaventure* began life as an impulse-driven (galactic-survey perhaps) disc to which the newly perfected warp drive was added ("installed")—an event occurring almost a century before *STTMP*, according to Gene Roddenberry's novelization. This design proved so practical that all Earth's major starships would copy it for the next two hundred years or more.

As misunderstood as the impulse drive has been the lowly shuttlecraft. Shuttlecraft have been deemed sublight from everyone from Franz Joseph to Wesley Crusher, though each successive generation has carried warp engines of the same distinctive design as its mother ship—from the cylindrical, half-ball-sterned nacelles of the original *Galileo* to the flattened, blue-rimmed engines of Picard's *Sakharov*, to the "movie style" warp pods of the *Galileo* and *Copernicus* in *The Final Frontier*.

Nor is this all: shuttlecraft missions have reflected hyperlight capability as well. Lokai stole a Starbase shuttlecraft some weeks before the events of "Let This Be Your Last Battlefield"; it is ludicrous to imagine he spent that time traveling laboriously to another planet of the same star system, from which he could have been readily extradited or recovered by another of the Starbase's vessels. Harry Mudd stole an armored shuttle in "Mudd's Passion" and put down on the sole desolated planet of an uncharted system; he could only have meant to wait out the ensuing search and then travel elsewhere. *Galileo* herself was shown in the course of an interstellar journey at the start of "Metamorphosis"; she was later tracked by her trail of "antimatter residue," a sure tip-off of warp engines. Kirk and an ersatz Mendez set out in pursuit of the *Enterprise*, suspecting it to be bound for Talos IV, four days distant from Starbase 11 at "maximum warp"—an effort they surely would not have made had their shuttlecraft been sublight ("The Menagerie"). *Copernicus* passed and then diverted into the Beta Lyrae system in "The Slaver Weapon," sporting warp pods equipped not just with the distinctive "exhausts" of the original and animated series, but with twin dorsal "intercoolers" as well. Finally, *The Next Generation* shuttle of "Samaritan's Snare" cannot have been conducting an hours-long sublight voyage to Starbase Scylla, since to let a shuttle off within light-hours of its destination represents little or no savings of time to a hyperlight Starship—a vessel shown, at last, to have been so close to the Starbase as to be able to reach it in time to save Picard's life when he was dying on the operating table. Only if the shuttle were able to travel light-years would it have made sense to use it. Wesley's disparaging "not exactly warp drive" can therefore only have meant "not exactly warp drive as we are accustomed to it aboard the *Enterprise*" (shuttlecraft may be capable of warp three or four, at most).

On occasion, shuttlecraft might be used to avoid the danger or disorientation of *near warp transport*—a beaming conducted, as in "The Schizoid Man," immediately upon a ship leaving warp. Presumably the effects of *downwarping* upon beaming persist for a matter of minutes, at least (else *Enterprise* would simply have waited for them to subside before dispatching the away team). Possibly the original *Enterprise*'s warp engines had no such side effect—but that any warp drive has indicates a little suspected aspect of transporter operation. It is popularly believed that the transportees' atoms are "scrambled about like a radio message," as

McCoy is wont to complain, but if this is so, why should downwarping cause any interference? Moreover, if the transporter so radically manipulates matter, why is it not a part of sickbay? It has, after all, been seen to make the old young again ("The Lorelei Signal," "Unnatural Selection"), split a man in two and make him whole again ("The Enemy Within"), even to change transportees' size ("The Terratin Incident," "The Counter-Clock Incident"). We have been told that such medicinal transport is both difficult and dangerous—that much energy is required, and that transportees risk having their bodies broken up and scattered inextricably through space. Not that such would matter to the dying, but why should it occur? Given a transport pattern of, one would think, virtual perfection, why should alteration of that pattern be any harder than its replication? To beam an object like a radio wave, the transporter would have to record and reproduce the position and makeup of every molecule. Why then could it not alter these in a controlled fashion?

The *matter/energy scrambler* transport principle says that it could—but we know that the transporter is not used for the duplication or creation of objects ("The Enemy Within" notwithstanding). Another device, the *replicator*, does this—and takes all the power of the warp engines to do it ("The Child"). *Holodeck matter*, although "created" by a transporter-like process, apparently requires constant application of power to exist; outside the holodeck it is unstable and rapidly dematerializes (with the occasional exception, perhaps, of water, snow, and paper, such as that on which "Moriarty" drew the *Enterprise*).

What then is the transporter, that it can move an object but only with great difficulty change its form? A clue is offered by the experience of transportees while beaming, as shown in both the films and the original series. *The Wrath of Khan* marked the introduction of speech and movement during transport, but series transportees were at least aware of the process of beaming, though apparently paralyzed. This is evident in Kirk's immediate call to the ship to inquire why beaming has failed in "The Apple"—a call too quickly made to have been an "I'm still here" response; he must have perceived the failure to dematerialize as his occurred. Ensign Garrovick too experienced the beaming process: on emerging from the difficult "cross-circuiting to B" recovery in "Obsession," he nervously clenched his fists, as if reassuring himself he really made it. Transportees are even seen to move their eyes during the onset of beaming in "That Which Survives," reacting to the arrival of Losira aboard ship.

None of these behaviors are the characteristics of radio messages, or of persons becoming same. We may conclude that the transporter is a space-warp phenomenon, perhaps involving, at its onset and conclusion, a nearly instantaneous conversion of matter to energy, then back to matter, prior to the transport (via space warp) itself. Matter/energy scrambler, indeed—little wonder warp drive interferes with it.

Finally, let us take up the matter of *warp speed*. The *Enterprise* of *The Next Generation* can reach a maximum of warp ten, though even that of the films is said to be faster (warp twelve, according to the *STTMP* blueprints). It has been said that this represents a redefinition on Gene Roddenberry's part of what Star Trek "really" is (like *STTMP*'s "this is what the Klingons really look like" revelation), but we may ignore this, even if it is true, since the new *Enterprise*'s velocities are obviously rated in *trans*warp factors (she operates in concert with Excelsior-class vessels, after all). But what speeds do such factors represent?

The new series writers' guide says that at warp six a ship travels a light-year an hour (a rate reflected in the time needed to return from Triangulum in "Where No One Has Gone Before"), while in "Q Who?" the time cited to go seven thousand light-years at maximum warp indicates a speed one-third as great—but neither of these figures makes sense. The old *Enterprise* went several times to the galaxy's edge (not to mention once to its core, an achievement erased from record or memory in light of *The Final Frontier*), which would take three years at an hour a light-year. Clearly, she must have traveled far faster, and Picard's *Enterprise* must be faster still. But how fast?

The original series writers' guide presented the formula "warp factor cubed, times light speed," which also yields years-long travel times to the galactic edge, but episodes tell a different story. In "That Which Survives," Spock said that the *Enterprise* could cross 990.7 light-years in 11.377 hours at warp 8.4. Dividing the warp-factor-cubed travel time by the actual time gives a correlation factor of 1292.4318. Applying this to other warp factors not only yields reasonable transit times to the galactic rim (thirty-five days at warp six), it makes sense of other feats of speed on the part of the *Enterprise* as well. In "Bread and Circuses," Chekov says of a planet, "Only one-sixteenth of a parsec away

. . . we should be there in seconds"—an impossibility at any "classical" warp value, but readily attainable at the revised warp five. Similarly rationalized is Admiral Barstow's order that all Starfleet forces withdraw to a hundred parsecs from the *Enterprise* in "The Alternative Factor"—hardly a practical command were classical warp speeds the norm. But what does this say of Picard's *Enterprise*?

An answer can be obtained from those cases in which the *Enterprise*'s attained warp speed did not match the revised formula. These include the intergalactic travel times of "By Any Other Name" and "Where No One Has Gone Before"; the complaints made by Kirk and Spock over three- and eight-light-year course diversions in "The Conscience of the King"; and Chekov's report that the *Enterprise* cannot afford a diversion of 2.8 light-days to Vulcan, lest she be late arriving at Altair ("Amok Time"). In these cases, use of the classical warp factor is implied. Clearly, warp speed must vary depending upon a ship's position within (or outside) the galaxy. Most likely this occurs due to minute changes in space mass density. Between galaxies, in the rifts between galactic arms, or in "star deserts" such as that of "Squire of Gothos," warp values drop to their classic values. Elsewhere, they are far higher (though intra-Federation travel times of months, as cited in "The Icarus Factor," may indicate that the prodigious performance of "That Which Survives" is rare). As for the transwarp speeds of the twenty-fourth-century *Enterprise*, we will note only that an hour a light-year is equal to a classical warp twenty. If the same correction factor operates upon transwarp, transwarp factor six is three seconds per light-year. If transwarp factors six and ten observed the same ratio as warp factors six and ten, transwarp ten is some six times as fast: two light-years a second.

Thus ends a brief trip through the technological wilderness of the Star Trek universe, a place not so simple as when Gene Roddenberry made a pilot the network rejected as too cerebral, and renamed lasers *phasers* for the remake. Today's Star Trek must include seventy-nine original series episodes, twenty-two animateds, five films, and three seasons of the new series to date. Star Trek's "facts" represent a "reality" which ship and crew often seem, eerily, more aware of than the very series creators. It is a reality not for the faint-hearted, but a reality that brooks no refutation. I will remain, like the inspiration that is the show itself, when all Star Trek's modern makers have passed on. As we must not fail the promise, let us not lose the helm.

Riker: "Increase to warp six.

LaForge: "Aye, sir. Full impulse."

"Conspiracy"

THE DISAPPEARING BUM—A FUN LOOK AT TIME TRAVELS IN STAR TREK

by Jeff Mason

"Everybody remember where we parked."

Jim and his shipmates left the park and entered the city at dawn. The sun burnished adobe houses with gold and burned away the fog. Long, fuzzy shadows shortened and sharpened.

Jim had not walked through his adopted home in a long while. Climbing the steep hills, he began to wish he had come on the voyage in a pair of good walking shoes instead of dress boots.

Ground cars and pedestrians crowded the streets and sidewalks. Jim's tension doubled as everyone around them gave them more than a second look. His group was suddenly surrounded by a forest of pointed fingers and running people. Spock, in particular, seemed to receive special notice. Jim's alarm grew; the rest looked bewildered as a crowd formed a tight circle, pushing and shouting good-natured gibberish. More people got out of ground cars, some of the vehicles stopping so fast that only luck prevented several minor accidents. Others ran weaving through traffic to join the swelling mob.

A small notepad and what Jim assumed to be a

writing instrument were shoved into his hands. Behind him, the others, too, were under a barrage of paper, everything from bound books to paper satchels. At the same time they were bombarded with unintelligible questions, to which they responded with a blank look or "Eh?" "Um?" or "Er?" To Jim, his crew looked to be more frightened by this than by any of the space monsters they'd faced or combat situations they'd been through together.

A long-haired, pimply youth popped up through the human wall and managed a reasonable facsimile of the Vulcan nerve pinch on the shoulder of a startled Spock.

"Live long and prosper, man!" the youngster said with a smile and a Vulcan salute.

Spock gently pushed away a small book called *Come Be With Me* proffered by another hand, and arched an eyebrow at Kirk.

"Fascinating."

The crowd around him laughed and clapped.

Kirk, not knowing what else to do, agreed with a young woman that his costume was indeed "authentic-looking," and then signed his name "James T. Kirk." The woman looked delighted.

Then the questions poured down on his head.

I've just written a revised version of a portion of Chapter 6 of Vonda McIntyre's novelization of *Star Trek IV: The Voyage Home*. I won't apologize. I'm just using it as an example to point out what would seem to be an obvious problem:

Just where the heck is *the* star trek in Star Trek? Where's the show, the movies, the entire sub-culture that grew around the Great Bird's creation? In all of the episodes or movies or novels that present Captain Kirk's past—our present—everything is exactly the same as in our reality, except for that one important cultural artifact: Star Trek. One of the most important and influential television shows in history is missing in Kirk's past. The mob scene I invented did not take place in McIntyre's novel, but why did it not take place?

In the first two editions of *The Best of Trek*, James Houston, Walter Irwin, and Mark Andrew Golding fought a very technical skirmish over the mechanics of time and time travel in the Star Trek universe. I get out of my depth very quickly in some of their arguments, especially those of Mr. Golding, but the ones I was able to wade through made it obvious that one of the major unsolved issues left alive after a run through the idea mill was the question of whether the Star Trek universe is one that runs on linear time, where events follow one after the other, unchanging and unchangeable, or if the Star Trek universe runs on time lines, those devices beloved of science fiction writers, in which time can be split into multiple realities by events called cusps.

Time lines are a lot more fun, as they can be split like firewood, tied or looped in fancy knots like ribbon, or erased altogether in mind-scrambling paradoxes in which you end up swallowed by scabrous green genealogical beasties of your own making. Under the rule of time-lines, Adolf Hitler could just as easily have been blown into a thousand oily pieces in the trenches of World War I as he could have become a frustrated artist who emigrates to America as he could have been dictator of Germany.

The absence of Star Trek the television show in the 1987 depicted in *Star Trek IV: The Voyage Home* conclusively proves the parallel-time-line theory of the Star Trek universe. If this is the case, then there must have been a cusp event that split our reality (hereafter called time line 1) from the "reality" that will become the universe in which the United Federation of Planets will exist, what we fans call the Star Trek Universe.

During the entire run of the TV series, and in all of the films, there is no mention that anyone else has attempted time travel to visit Earth's past. Therefore, I contend that the split between time line 1 and time line 2 was caused by the inadvertent intervention and/or outright carelessness of the crew of the *Enterprise.*

The crew is well aware that critical cusps affecting time don't have to be major, earth-shaking events—Edith Keeler proved that to them. But could something else just as seemingly minor, perhaps even more so, have caused a cusp that would, amazingly, protect the founding of the Federation by destroying its TV image in the twentieth century?

In "Tomorrow Is Yesterday," Kirk gets an A in temporal damage control; no new time lines were created. But as no one recognized him as a member of the *Enterprise,* we may assume that the split took place earlier than the 1960s. The same thing is true of "Assignment: Earth." Therefore, we must look to the earliest time to which the *Enterprise* crew traveled: the 1930s of "City on the Edge of Forever."

Throughout the episode Kirk and Spock work to identify and fix the damage done to time by McCoy in his drug-induced madness. The cusp, of course, is the life or death of Edith Keeler: If she lives, the Federation is washed from time's blackboard; if she dies, Kirk's and Spock's future is guaranteed. In this case history is like a time-line marshaling yard: it's up to Kirk and Spock to guide the train onto the right branch line before McCoy arrives and slides it onto a dead-end siding. Kirk, at immense cost to himself, rights the wrong to history. They return to their present, appearing to have corrected every change in the time line that has been caused by their presence.

Or have they?

There is one event, caused also by McCoy's intervention, that is *not* rectified when the trio returns through the Portal. This event is odd in that it seems to have no relation to the other happenings in the episode. It occurs, and nothing that follows appears affected by it. But it seems McCoy inadvertently found a new branch siding and switched the temporal express right onto it.

Scene: McCoy has just crossed through the Guardian. The first person he sees in the streetlamp light is a bum, a nobody like thousands of others belched out of the guts of the Great Depression. His evening meal is in his hand. McCoy screams and rages, obviously out of his mind, so the bum freezes, hoping the madman will just walk back through the wall again.

He stands petrified as the doctor questions him and examines his skull, then stands surprised as the crazy collapses in a gibbering heap. He gets over his astonishment fast enough to rifle the pockets of the unconscious lunatic. He doesn't find any recognizable swag, but comes up with an oblong black box that fits nicely in his hand. The vagrant doesn't know what it is, but he's sure he can sell it downtown for next week's flophouse money. But first, what do these buttons do?

A bright, human-shaped glow and the bum is dead, atomized. Another nexus has been created, another fork in time that can't be fixed because even McCoy doesn't remember it happening. Even Edith's later death doesn't change this one. To show how important this is, we'll look at the original problem created by McCoy's rescue of Miss Keeler.

Only two time lines are involved so far. If Edith lives, the pacifist movement she leads in the U.S. permits the Nazis to win World War II with atomic weapons; the Federation is prevented from existing on that line. If Edith dies, history should follow its familiar channel. Familiar in this case includes the airing of Star Trek the television series from 1966 to 1969. This causes a problem.

If Star Trek is allowed to exist on the time line that will eventually produce the Federation, the very existence of the show and subculture in the twentieth century will paradoxically negate the universe of the *Enterprise* that we are familiar with in the twenty-third, as modeling an interplanetary government and defense force on a three-hundred-year-old video show would be considered ridiculous. The Federation might exist on such a line, but its form and name would be radically changed. Another break in the time stream must have happened to create both our time line and the *Enterprise*'s line 2.

When Kirk lets Edith die, he thinks he is preserving the integrity of time line 1, the prime line. But even as she becomes one with the pavement, they are all unaware that they are riding on time line 2, which I argue was born with the death of that nameless bum.

Jim's subsequent actions here are understandable:

He is so distraught at the loss of Edith, and so relieved to have restored the time fabric at the same time, that his judgment and command faculties are not at their best. But it still remains that he failed to examine their actions completely to ensure no other damage was done, and if found, to somehow prevent that bum's death from the overlooked phaser blast. Therefore, if Edith's end creates two possibilities, two separate lines, McCoy's accidental killing of the bum creates *four* different potential realities.

One: The bum is killed. Edith is hit by that truck. Result, Nazis lose, Federation comes into being.

Two: Bum dies. Edith lives (we assume that Kirk is unable to prevent McCoy from saving her, or that Jim cannot allow her to die). Nazis win, Federation winks out.

Three: Bum lives (does not find phaser or does not experiment with any buttons). Edith dies, Nazis lose, Federation is founded.

Four: Bum lives. Edith is saved by that dashing young captain from the future. Hitler takes it all, Kirk and Edith die in nuclear strike on New York City in 1943. Spock ends his days repairing mechanical rice pickers, and McCoy goes to work on the railway. (I *am* an engineer, not a doctor!) Federation dies a horrible temporal death, squeezed off into more exotic dimensions.

Fine. By the above list it seems it doesn't matter doodly squat whether the bum glows in the dark or not. But it stands that Star Trek the series, the movies, the throngs of Trekkers would track down and corner Kirk, Spock, and the others at penpoint were they to show up in the San Francisco of 1986 (or the

1968 of "Assignment: Earth"), do not exist on Kirk's time line 2.

I'm going to engage in speculation, whether you like it or not. I mentioned earlier that the bum was heretofore unnamed, so let's call him George. The fact that George dies because, and only because, of McCoy seems important. What happened as a result of his "untimely" demise?

We can guess that George was one of many unemployed workers with a family to support, as he is middle-aged and most likely married. Stealing and begging to try to feed his children became his full-time job. In spite of this he would try to be a good father, and inspire in his kids hope for the good times he remembers, and that will come again. We can say his children loved him and leaned on him a great deal, as George drew support from them.

One, a boy in his early adolescence, is shattered by his father's sudden disappearance. Not knowing of George's death, he comes to the conclusion that he and his siblings are victims of desertion. He grows resentful and rebellious.

The young man is drafted in 1942, but is given a dishonorable discharge for a drunken attack on an officer. He then wanders from one menial job to another, finally falling onto the welfare rolls.

In 1953, after an epic pub crawl on the last of his welfare money, George's son runs down and kills a police sergeant in Los Angeles. No one saw the late-night hit-and-run, and the drunk speeds off, driving until he runs out of gas. A few years later, still in fear of being caught, he dies of alcohol poisoning in a Chicago hospital.

So? It happens that that policeman in his spare time moonlighted as a television scriptwriter, one who was getting very good at what he did. His name was Gene Roddenberry.

Thus, Star Trek would have never been shown. It is not exaggeration to say that without the social impetus of the idealism behind the show, concern for the environment and other aspects of the human condition would be blunted. Interest in the space program, acceptance of space-oriented research, or pursuit of any outward-looking policy was discouraged. The pessimism of the Sixties generated by the Vietnam War, and the worldwide invitation to a nuclear barbecue, was not countered by the optimism and hope generated by the original voyages of the *Enterprise*, and by Roddenberry's own world vision. This mood was not helped any by the syndication and endless reruns of *Lost in Space*.

In TV and perhaps elsewhere, racial integration would have been set back years, as well as concern for endangered species like humpback whales, all in part due to the absence of Roddenberry's ground-breaking. This is the reality of time line 2, a world exactly like ours except without Star Trek, all resulting from the accidental death of a bum in the 1930s. This cusp is just as important as Edith's death, and in conjunction with it gives new importance to the four separate time lines I listed before. We'll look at them again.

One: The bum is killed. Edith dies as well. The show Star Trek does not air. Lack of ecological concern helps humpbacked whales as well as other animals to become extinct. The Federation is established, and the *Enterprise* undertakes its famous and well-documented five-year mission. Add Eugenics wars, Colonel Green, Tribbles, Klingons, etc., shake well, and you've got time line 2.

Two: The bum is vaporized but Edith lives. The Nazis use A-bombs to conquer the world. Presumably the whales die out and in consequence the probe destroys a planet full of fifteenth-generation National Socialists.

For obvious reasons Star Trek never aired on this line, as the state-run stations only showed the *Adolf and Eva Variety Hour*.

Three: The bum doesn't find the phaser and survives. Edith becomes a New York City traffic statistic. The Allies whip the Hun. The Great Bird of the Galaxy, alias Gene Roddenberry, produces his cult favorite from 1966 to 1969. The humpbacks manage to survive, albeit in small numbers. A body that might well vaguely resemble the Federation could be down the road, but there is not a recognizable *Enterprise* and James T. Kirk winds up as captain of the Saturn-Earth tourist shuttle.

This is our reality, time line 1.

Four: George lives to scrounge another day, and Edith is saved just in time. The landing party on the Guardian's planet, desperate for food, wind up eating (who else?) the hapless security men. Otherwise, treat as Two above.

Note in only one of the possibilities does Roddenberry get to make Star Trek. This is also the line on which is the greatest possibility of survival for the whales: therefore on line 1, the probe will not need to pencil in a side trip to Earth. If McCoy's phaser had *not* done in the vagrant and Edith *had* died, Kirk, Spock, and

McCoy would have gone back through the portal to find themselves still in a choronological mess, except this time they'd be on line 1, no *Enterprise*, an unrecognizable Federation-like organization, and a Saturn-bound shuttle with a missing captain. But when the Guardian told Kirk everything was back the way it was, it knew of what it spoke. McCoy *had* to cause George the Bum's death in order for the following cusp of Edith's death to have its desired effect.

Because the crew of the *Enterprise* never journeyed further in the past than the 1930s, we can assume that as far as the Federation is concerned, before George's death time was running on only one major line (all other cusps of importance happening so far in the past that they resulted in alien realities, as would have occurred if for some unknown reasons Europeans had never colonized the New World). If you accept this, it follows that McCoy as a matter of historical continuity *had* to inject himself with cordrazine in order to charge through the Portal and effect the change that would ensure the future of the Federation on line 2. The reality of the *Enterprise* and its universe could not stand it otherwise. The cusps McCoy provoked had to happen in their particular sequence for the future to remain as he remembered it, George's death being in this case just as important as Edith's.

The irony of this, of course, is that by saving the Federation, by destroying Star Trek, and condemning the whales, McCoy has guaranteed the deadly visit of the probe, which requires that he and his friends once again use time travel to save their future reality.

This is all supposition, of course, but in order for everything to return to the way it originally was, as the

Guardian saw it, the bum's killing was a vital necessity. Otherwise, at the end of "City," the Guardian wouldn't have told the captain that everything was patched up again. (It would have told the captain, in that dignified ten-commandments voice, that McCoy had fumbled the goose pâté again, and with whipped-puppy expressions the trio would have trooped dutifully back through the gateway to try it one more time.)

While this argument may not have the number-rattling, theory-twisting complexity of Mr. Golding's or Mr. Irwin's, it proves the time-line theory of the Star Trek universe. It can be seen that the show does not exist in the realities that Kirk visits in the past, and I assert the reason for this is the death of George, the unsung bum. This death spawned two different time lines, ours and the *Enterprise*'s.

I leave it to the experienced Star Trek authors to come up with some interesting plots involving the two lines, something gauche involving the return to kill Gene to save the future . . . or maybe a plot line that's a little more elegant, as in . . . I know, Jim and Spock masquerading as NBC executives in 1964, discouraging a hopeful Gene Roddenberry from developing his really neat idea for a "Wagon Train to the Stars":

Kirk adjusted the uncomfortably thick glasses on his nose and fingered the thick manuscript. An anxious Roddenberry looked on.

"It'll never fly. Nobody would believe it. Right, Mister, er . . . Spocknik?"

Spock stopped trying to perfect his necktie knot. "Check, Capta—Chief."

HUMANISM IN STAR TREK—
AN ALTERNATIVE APPROACH

by Ron Beshears

The appearance of the article "Mythology and the Bible in Star Trek" in *The Best of Trek #8* and *#9* has prompted me to write an article in response, in which I wish to address some points of that article, as well as make a few points from a perspective largely ignored in previous articles.

My major complaint with the aforementioned article is that it states in several places that the biblical account of the history of mankind is accurate and truthful. Statements such as "Jesus is real and divine" and "God is everywhere" on the part of the authors leave little room for interpretation. It is clear that these authors fully believe these doctrines and expect the general reader to as well. I found numerous points of contention in the article (which I will not go into boring detail about at this point, although I can if that is requested), most of which have to do with attempts by the authors to square biblical accounts with recorded events in history, or to load down characters and events in the Star Trek universe with supposed parallels to characteristics of Christian faith.

Further, I will not deal with the nature of attacks by

so-called "brothers in Christ" on humanism as a doctrine of thought which are so prevalent in society today, and which are implied in a few places in the article I am responding to. That article contains many pretentious assurances of "God's power" and "God's mercy" which, after careful rereading, begin to seem little more than shameless sermonizing. Rather than attempt to foist personal beliefs on you, the reader, I wish to expose you in as unbiased a manner as possible to an alternative point of view, and leave you free to draw your own conclusions, without airing my views concerning the question of the existence of a supreme being.

Being a physicist by trade and a humanist in matters of personal philosophy, my views of life and of Star Trek are likely to be somewhat different than those of the typical fan. Perhaps the way to begin is to quote a definition of humanism (as a philosophy), as defined by the American Humanist Association:

Humanism is optimistic regarding human nature and confident in human reason and science as the best means of reaching the goal of human fulfillment in this world. Humanists affirm that humans are a product of the same evolutionary process that produced all other living organisms and that all ideas, knowledge, values, and social systems are based upon human experience. Humanists conclude that creative ability and personal responsibility are strongest when the mind is free from supernatural belief and operates in an atmosphere of freedom and democracy.

Admittedly, this pocket definition is short and a bit formal, but it serves adequately for the purpose of this discussion. One immediate precept that can be inferred from the definition is that humanists strive to respect other individuals as much as is practically possible. This theme is abundantly obvious in Star Trek; most of the episodes carried the message that any life form, no matter how alien or unusual, deserved at least some measure of respect and considerate treatment. Even the villains of Star Trek were generally shown to have (but not *always* shown to have) qualities and motivations that could be respected to some degree, even if we begrudged them those qualities or questioned their motivations.

This is a rather far cry from the rather superstitious fear and hatred of perceived threats to Christian faith (i.e., "The devil is the deceiver," the mythology article proclaims, and one gets the feeling that "Klingons-Devils" is a fairly accurate statement to infer from the attitude of the authors). Well, of course the Klingons are deceivers, not to mention murderers and marauders. Despite these facts, however, it has been amply demonstrated that the Klingons possess technological skills, knowledge of strategy, and some measure of intelligent thinking ability. As much as we may resent the Klingons, those qualities demand respect and consideration in their own right. Also, the Klingons have motivations for their behavior that to them are quite logical and reasonable.

Rather than comparing Klingons to the primitive biblical superstition of Gog and Magog, I feel that a far more telling comparison is that of the years-long situation between the United States and the Soviet Union.

Americans fear and mistrust the government of the Soviet Union, and not without reason. However, intelligent Americans also have a measure of respect for the abilities of the Soviet government, grudging respect perhaps but respect nonetheless. It is this respect that offers some hope for humanity. People who proudly display their "Russia Sucks" bumper stickers, and their ideological cousins who insist on imposing their religious tenets on the public at large, are never going to help us in reaching the ideas of the Star Trek universe.

As long as people concentrate on stirring the flames of nationalism and supremist religious attitudes, mankind will never successfully mount a permanent presence in space, since each nationalistic/ideological faction will be too busy competing with all the others to devote its resources to the goals of meaningful space exploration. The history of our own nation makes this point painfully obvious. Mankind will establish the ability to travel in space as he is shown traveling in Star Trek only when he has left behind his primitive nationalism and ideologies and devotes the energies of the finest minds available on Earth to solve the problems of interstellar travel, rather than devoting them to finding new weapons with which to eliminate one another.

A unified world democratic society with freedom of behavior and belief is what I am implying here, and it is exactly this kind of society that Star Trek proposes as the society of Earth in the twenty-third century. In fact, specific references to the society of Earth are made in a number of the episodes, and the general trend of these remarks indicates that the Earth of Star Trek's time is a society in which discrimination and persecution are frowned upon as primitive, childish attitudes, and in which individualism and respect for personal rights and qualities are among mankind's highest qualities. Individuals are *free* to be individuals in the Star Trek universe; they are not fearful of what they are and feel no need for conformism. Also, they sorely resent attempts by outside parties to control their freedom of action and thought.

Humanists also have a high regard for the scientific/technical professions, and are confident that it is these professions which will provide humanity with the answers it needs to exist in the future. The very concept of Star Trek is based on this idea. The *Enterprise*, at least in Gene Roddenberry's original conception, was a device provided by the technology of the future to be used by mankind and allied life forms to explore and attempt to understand the universe they observed around them.

In point of fact, many of the series episodes deviated from the original idea at least to some extent, but this is simply because scientific research doesn't always provide exciting story elements (a fact I know from personal experience). Star Trek was a vision of mankind truly in his element—taking risks in the unknown regions of the universe in order to satisfy an insatiable curiosity that is as inherent in mankind as is the need to keep breathing in order to survive. The characters of the series applied science and reason to their problems in order to understand and solve them, and thereby kept on surviving so that they might be able to keep on exploring. This is the hope of humanism—that mankind will eventually have the ability *and* freedom to express and satisfy that inherent curiosity in an unrestricted manner.

Several episodes of Star Trek attempted to express this hope for the future of humanity by showing the effects of restriction of thought and/or action in societies which were somewhat like that of present-day Earth in various ways. A few examples are the episodes "The Return of the Archons," "A Taste of Armageddon," "Patterns of Force," "Mirror, Mirror," and "Let That Be Your Last Battlefield." In these episodes, the issues of totalitarianism, nationalism, and prejudice were plainly exposed, and in each case were judged and found to be wanting. Each of these problems is abundant in the society of Earth, and it was the message of these episodes that these problems must be overcome in order for humanity to achieve those goals that are set in the vision of Star Trek.

Humanism also dismissed belief in supernatural beings, and this is a point that several episodes probed gently but never approached at face value, with the possible exception of *Star Trek: The Motion Picture*. Despite its flaws that movie was a unified vision of the future evolution of mankind, and this vision was related to the viewer with no attempts to resort to a supernatural belief system. Many viewers (and, sadly, many Star Trek fans as well) did not understand or accept this idea because it conflicted with their conscious or subconscious religious attitudes.

Many episodes dealt with belief systems of various societies, and for the most part these episodes were enlightening as well as entertaining in that they provided insights into the structure of religious thought and the influence—both positive and negative—of religion in a culture.

Only one episode approached the level of openly preaching the Christian message to the viewer, and that only at the end of the episode. That episode, of course, was "Bread and Circuses," which is generally regarded by most fans as one of Star Trek's better episodes. That episode did deal positively with the idea that religious persecution is just as bad as any other form, but it was disappointing to see James Kirk delivering a sermonette at the end of the episode which advocated only the Christian point of view.

Another episode which explored religious beliefs in some detail was "Who Mourns for Adonais," which advanced the theory that Apollo and the other gods of the Greek/Roman belief system (commonly referred to by Christians in a disdainful tone as "polytheism" or "pagan religion") were in fact humanoid life forms whose superior technological skills intimidated the early civilizations into worshiping them for their abilities and fearing actions which would incur their wrath. The conclusion of the episode attempted to show that intimidation is not reason to suppress or sacrifice one's individuality and thinking ability in order to conform to a religious attitude. This story dealt explicitly with the legend of Apollo, but it could easily have dealt with the legend of the Christian God or the legend of Jesus Christ.

I realize that the use of the word *legend* at this point is very controversial, and I feel it necessary to justify my choice of words. The beliefs of the ancient Greeks and Romans were found to be based only on myth, legend, and exaggerated stories several centuries ago.

However, this does not make that belief structure any better or worse than any other structure.

Admittedly, the accounts of events in the Bible are self-consistent and well organized to a fairly high degree, but this in no way supports their authenticity. It is true that several books of the New Testament contain statements by various disciples that the accounts contained therein are truthful and accurate, but these statements are of no value or significance in weighing the question of whether the events described there actually took place in human history. A well-written novel is self-consistent and contains numerous self-references that all fit together to make a convincing story, but that does not change the fact that the events of the story are pure fiction. I am *not* implying with this statement that the Bible is a novel, and that inference should *not* be drawn by readers of this article. I am only pointing out the fact that self-consistency is not adequate evidence of authenticity.

On that basis, the story of Christ is no more or less believable than the story of Apollo or any other legendary character. At this point, Christians will resort to stating that faith in God and Christ provides evidence of authenticity and proves that their worldview is the only right one. Well, faith in Apollo was all the Greeks and Romans needed to prove to themselves the authenticity and correctness of their own belief system. What I am pointing out is that faith in any legendary character, without the availability of even a small bit of incontrovertible physical evidence on which to base that faith, is resolutely illogical.

The message to religious people that should be evident from this discussion is this: If your religious belief system works for you, for whatever reasons, fine. Keep on professing your belief and practicing your religion, because that is your right as a human. However, have enough respect for the rest of humanity to be mindful that some people have no need or reason to share your beliefs, and are annoyed and offended when you openly proclaim your personal feelings that your belief system is the right one and that those of us who do not agree are consigned to eternal damnation.

This is the message, although not so clearly defined, that is the underlying theme of the Star Trek episodes that dealt with religious beliefs. It is this simple respect for one another that humanism is attempting to teach and it is this respect that will be necessary for humanity to reach the future that Star Trek promises.

This respect must also be accorded to whatever alien life forms—whether benevolent or malignant—that humanity may encounter in the future. Instead of trying to eliminate the difference humans see in one another and in whatever life is "out there" (in the words of James Kirk), we should appreciate and celebrate, for it is those differences that make life an adventure instead of a crashing bore. It is this line of reasoning that produced the concept of the Vulcan philosophy of IDIC—Infinite Diversity in Infinite Combinations— which was introduced in the episode "Is There in Truth No Beauty?" (perhaps the only positive contribution that particular episode ever made to the Star Trek universe). The Vulcans, logical and rational beings that they are, apparently realized that diversity is that quality which defines the course of life and sets us all apart from one another, and that diversity is therefore deserving of high respect.

The Vulcan philosophy of IDIC is in many ways a mirror image of the philosophy of humanism, and it is high time that humanism is appreciated on that level rather than being used as a scapegoat by religious fanatics in their criticism of so-called "secular humanism" as the root cause of all the evils they perceive in the world around them. Humanism is considerate enough to tolerate their belief systems, while not agreeing with them. It is only fair that religious people recognize their responsibility to extend this same amount of respect to their fellow humans.

This is among the highest of the ideals of Star Trek, and should be promoted as an ideal of humanity in our time. The future can only be a good one if humanity is willing to work in concert to make it so. Science fiction writers are well known for writing stories which present a grim, dirty view of the future of Earth, and several of these stories have made it to the big screen (for example, *Blade Runner* and the Mad Max series). A careful combination of the sketchy details of the "future history" given in these stories invariably shows that hatred and prejudice were at the basis of the events which led to the condition of human society as presented in these stories.

Star Trek, on the other hand, presents an optimistic view of humanity, and expresses confidence in our ability to overcome our primitive attitudes and reach the stars. It clearly indicates, however, that this bright future will only come about if we are willing to pay the price of daring to be individuals, and respecting the courage of others who have already dared to do so. The responsibility to produce the kind of future we see in Star Trek lies heavily upon the present generation, as technology is advancing more rapidly during our times than at any time in the past. That responsibility consists of educating ourselves and our children to know how to shape the future by taking advantage of the resources of technology and of human intellect and ability. Someone who believes that faster-than-light travel is impossible will certainly never find a way to accomplish it; similarly, someone who is resigned to the idea that the future will be grim and dirty will see exactly that kind of future, because he has no confidence in his own ability to exert influence on events in his life.

Star Trek fans are in an unusually advantageous position to act on this responsibility, since they have by and large accepted the message of Star Trek and are intrigued by the possibility of the future that Star Trek portrays. Therefore, my advice is twofold: First, continue to watch, read, and think about Star Trek (and if you are like me, you'll probably eat, sleep, and breathe Star Trek as well), because Star Trek provides you with a unique exposure to the highest ideals of humanity; and second, *act* on the dreams that Star Trek inspires in you.

THE GIANT
STAR TREK NOVEL

by Susan M. Steele

The giant Star Trek novel. Has a nice ring to it, doesn't it?

Giant implies something bigger, something better. The books themselves are still physically the same size, so giant must mean the story is better. At least, that's what it is supposed to mean.

After reading and pondering Pocket Books' first three giant Star Trek novels, I have come to a conclusion: A giant Star Trek novel is not that much different from a regular one. These giant Star Trek novels were all written by authors with previous Star Trek experience. *Enterprise*, published in September 1986, was written by Vonda McIntyre; *Strangers From the Sky*, by Margaret Wander Bonnano, was published in July 1987; and *The Final Frontier*, released in January 1988, was authored by Diane Carey. And even though these writers have all created new adventures for the *Enterprise* crew in the past, these supposedly giant adventures do not seem all that original.

And that is what this review comes down to, in large part: originality. While *Enterprise*, *Strangers*, and *Frontier* may be giant Star Trek novels, they really are not anything new. This article will examine in detail these three giant Star Trek novels and discuss why, in this case, bigger does not necessarily mean better.

Vonda McIntyre has had a substantial amount of previous experience with Star Trek novels. In 1981, her first Star Trek novel, *The Entropy Effect*, was published (it was Pocket Books' first original Star Trek novel). This was followed by her novelizations of *Star Trek II: The Wrath of Khan, Star Trek III: The Search for Spock*, and *Star Trek IV: The Voyage Home*.

The Entropy Effect was an interesting story about, of all things, the effect of entropy. It seems that with its effect, people are able to change the past, thus altering the future. In theory, one could go back and change one specific time line in several instances by interrupting the time line at different places. However, I felt the story was a bit too technical in that it required a slightly more than basic understanding of physics to grasp the concept of entropy.

As for the film novelizations, I tend to be a purist. I was a bit disappointed to find out that these adaptations are sometimes different from the finished movie because they are based on the original shooting script and not the final edited version of the film. The movies end up being shorter, more tightly sequenced, and seem much more intense on film, especially in the case of *Wrath of Khan*.

Margaret Wander Bonnano previously wrote *Dwellers in the Crucible* for Pocket Books in 1985. *Dwellers* was, for the most part, a gripping story. It involved the kidnapping of a group of people living on Vulcan to assure the peace of the Federation by the Klingons. Two of the Dwellers, both female, an outcast Vulcan and a sheltered Terran, become friends during their ordeal. The story is an interesting view of the Vulcan-human relationship. However, the story deals almost entirely with these two characters, and the roles of the *Enterprise* crew amount to almost cameos. The story takes a few strange plot twists near the end, but otherwise it is a touching story.

It was interesting to see the human-Vulcan relationship explored so deeply, but it would have been nice to see this relationship as applied to Kirk and Spock or, even better, McCoy and Spock, instead of two unknown characters. Again, I tend to be a purist. Remember, "These are the voyages of the starship *Enterprise* . . ." I prefer novels that include all of the *Enterprise* regulars as the focal point, with new characters making the guest appearances.

Diane Carey has also written for Star Trek previously. *Dreadnought* and *Battlestations* were both relatively good action-adventure stories. Written in the first person, the crew of the *Enterprise* is seen through the eyes of a young female officer named Piper. While both stories, taken on their own, are interesting, they actually are very similar. Both involve the theft of new technology (by someone who is up to no good, of course), and in both stories Piper is the key to the resolution of the problem. While I do feel that Piper is one of the most well developed of the non-regular characters, I am slightly put off by the lack of originality.

As for characterization, it is slightly better than Vonda McIntyre's, but not quite as good as Margaret Bonnano's. The only real problem is with Kirk. Piper is described as an attractive young woman, but Kirk never even gives her a second look. There is hardly a hint of attraction. While some may argue that Kirk has had his share of romances and Piper is a junior officer assigned to his ship, his complete indifference of her is somewhat out of character.

Now that we have established the credentials of the authors, it is time to take a detailed look at the giant Star Trek novels.

Enterprise, the first of them, relates Captain James T. Kirk's first voyage as commander of the *Enterprise*. Kirk has just broken off his relationship with Carol Marcus and his good friend, Gary Mitchell, is still seriously ill, recovering from an incident at Ghioghe. Unfortunately, Kirk does not hit it off too well with the rest of the crew. Commodore Pike, Lieutenant Uhura, Mister Scott, and Commander Spock all treat Starfleet's youngest starship captain like a child, and for most of the story Kirk has a hard time trying not to offend anyone. McCoy, already an old friend of Kirk's, seems the closest to the characterization we later know.

James Kirk's first assignment is to transport a vaudeville troupe on a performing tour to some of the outpost colonies. Our young captain is not, of course, too happy with the idea; he was hoping for something significantly more exciting. But he follows orders. As it turns out, the *Enterprise* does come across a new species of life and their world, and a few nasty Klingons thrown in for good measure. Not to diminish the resolution of the story, everything works out in the end.

While Vonda McIntyre has managed to write a mildly entertaining story, I find fault most with her characterizations. At this point in time, nearly everyone who reads Star Trek novels knows the characters inside and out. Today's Star Trek writer must consider characterization to be one of the most—if not *the* most—important factors in a novel. No matter how good a plot is, if a writer has the characters saying and doing things that you, the reader, know they would not normally say or do, the story loses some of its impact.

In this case, Ms. McIntyre does have some leeway. She was writing about the characters at a time before we knew them as they are in the television series. However, from the references in *Enterprise*, we can estimate that the story is set at a time (approximately) six to eighteen months before the time of "Where No Man Has Gone Before."

Of all the characters, I think Spock is written with the least believability. This is not entirely Ms. McIntyre's error. When we see Spock in "The Cage," he is almost more human than Vulcan. He is quite emotional, even smiling occasionally. This is to be expected because of his emotional conflict and the fact that he probably has not been in contact with humans for very long. And by the time the series started, Spock was actually much the same. It was several episodes into the series before he developed into the Mr. Spock we are familiar with. Then, in "The Menagerie," we learn that he served with Captain Pike for more than ten years. Obviously there is a conflict here, as it appears that Spock, who was so emotional serving under Captain Pike, suddenly becomes more Vulcan when serving under Captain Kirk.

Ms. McIntyre chooses to get around this conflict by making Spock almost completely emotionless, even though the story is set at a time when we can presume that he would still have had some conflicts in his emotions and behavior. In *Enterprise*, Spock is seen as very stiff and proper, with absolutely no tolerance for Captain Kirk's youth and emotionalism. He even goes so far as to contemplate a transfer. After serving so long with Captain Pike, one would think he could at least be a little more tolerant.

Speaking of Captain Pike, he does not come off much better than Spock. The newly promoted Commodore Pike makes only a brief appearance in the story, but he is seen as cold, overbearing, and with no sympathy at all for Kirk's apprehension at taking over command of the *Enterprise*.

Kirk's characterization is not too far off the mark, but he seems slightly more awkward and unsure of himself than would be expected of a man who has already proven himself to be a hero at Axanar and has just been appointed as the youngest captain in Starfleet.

Sulu sulks through most of the story because he would rather be risking his life on the frontier than helming the *Enterprise*. Scotty thinks that Kirk is a young whippersnapper who does not know what he is doing. Chekov makes an appearance when he is not supposed to be on the ship for at least another two years, and ends up sounding like a Russian immigrant. Dr. McCoy seems to be much the same old country doctor we are used to, and Uhura and Rand are not that far off, either. The fact that both of these female characters, Rand especially, were not featured much in the series makes it easier for us to see them. In other words, we never got very close to them as characters in the series, so postulating their early years is easy.

In some ways, the story does reach the point it is trying to make: showing the familiar *Enterprise* crew before they were familiar to us (and to each other). On the other hand, the two basic plot devices in the story, a new civilization and Klingon aggressors, have both been used many times before. Janet Kagan and David Gerrold presented excellent stories on new species in their books, *Uhura's Song* and *The Galactic Whirlpool*, respectively. And the Klingons have been portrayed much better in the television series, especially in "Errand of Mercy" and "Day of the Dove." While *Enterprise* is by no means a poor story, something a little more original—as this is supposed to be the first mission of the famous *Enterprise* crew—may have been better in line with the giant story theme.

Strangers From the Sky is not exactly a story that lends itself well to summarization. In *Strangers*, Dr. McCoy is reading a new best-seller called *Strangers From the Sky*. He loves the book and gives it to Kirk to read. After Kirk reads the book, he begins having nightmares and believes that he knows, or should know, the characters and events in the book. Through an extended mind-meld with Spock, Kirk learns that he really was involved in that early human-Vulcan contact. Shortly before the events of "Where No Man Has Gone Before," Kirk, Spock, Gary Mitchell, Elizabeth Dehner, and Lee Kelso beam down to Planet M-155. While there, they are accidentally transported to Earth in the year 2045 and somehow stumble onto the fact that two aliens have been discovered and no one knows what to do with them.

After scattering themselves all over the globe, Kirk and his crew manage to rescue the Vulcans from the narrow-minded humans of twenty-first-century Earth and return to their own time. Coming out of the mind-meld, Kirk and Spock realize that the memory of the contact has been erased from their minds. It is only through reading the book "Strangers From the Sky," which gives a supposedly fictional account of the first human-Vulcan contact, that their memories are finally triggered.

I have touched only briefly on the true plot. Over the course of *Strangers*, James Kirk's sanity is questioned, Spock ends up meeting his great-great-grandfather in the past, and, once again, the Earth of the twenty-first century is shown to be prejudiced and fearful of alien life forms.

I must admit that the story is actually quite engrossing and Ms. Bonnano certainly knows her characters. She seems to have very little problem moving between the Kirk and Spock of an earlier day and the Kirk and Spock of the series. There are a few places where the story seems to take convenient turns. While in the year 2045, Kirk and his twenty-third-century crew seem to have very little problem adjusting to a totally different life-style, and even manage to split up and move all over Earth, taking on other identities, falsifying documents, and using cash. They also manage to outwit nearly every human on Earth, persuade one of the Vulcans that death is not the answer when it seems the end is near, and find a small, nuclear-powered ship to take the Vulcans back to their home. Spock, separated from the others, lives with an old recluse, and it turns out the man is his great-great-grandfather. Some of the plot twists are just a little too fantastic to be believed. And, of course, there is the idea that there was a human-Vulcan contact before the "official" one and the fact that Kirk and Spock were present.

On the whole, *Strangers* is an entertaining story that moves quickly. Compared to Ms. McIntyre, Ms. Bonnano definitely has a better handle on the characters, both in the past and in the present. Perhaps my only regret is that twenty-first-century humans are depicted as incredibly insular and fearful of aliens. It seems that whenever the *Enterprise* crew travels back in time, they are confronted by people who are highly prejudiced and paranoid: Kirk said as much in *The Voyage Home*. Maybe sometime someone will write a Star Trek story where twenty-first-century man or even twentieth-century man is more receptive to alien contact. Ms. Bonnano has also shown here her fascination with Vulcans. Because she is such an excellent author, it would be nice to see her do something a little different in her next Star Trek novel.

The Final Frontier is the most recent giant Star Trek novel. Unfortunately, it is far too similar to *Strangers From the Sky* to be taken seriously. *Frontier* relates the first human-Romulan contact at least twenty years before Kirk meets the Romulan commander in "Balance of Terror." Coming on the heels of *Strangers*, this book pales by comparison. The plots are nearly indistinguishable from each other.

Kirk's father, George Samuel Kirk, is assigned as the first officer on Starfleet's newest secret invention, the first starship. The captain of this as yet unnamed vessel is Robert April. The story unfolds as James T. Kirk returns home to Iowa after the tragic events of "City on the Edge of Forever." Kirk is mourning the loss of Edith Keeler and, sitting in the loft of the old barn, rereads the letters his father wrote to him and his brother when they were young. The story is actually in two parts: James Kirk reliving old memories and mourning present-day losses, and George Samuel Kirk's mission aboard the starship.

We learn that the starship (affectionately called "Empress" by both Kirk and April before being officially named) is needed on a rescue mission. It is the only ship that can reach a stranded vessel soon enough to save the passengers and crew from certain death. When engaging warp drive for the first time, the starship goes out of control and ends up in Romulan space, due to a Romulan conspirator aboard the ship. After a lengthy space battle and some serious, though heavy-handed, moral battles regarding the military and scientific aspects of the new vessel, the starship manages to return to Federation space with a helpful Romulan commander on board. The starship rescues the stranded vessel and the Romulan commander, now in exile, prepares for some cosmetic surgery.

First of all, human-Vulcan first contact is a viable story idea. We know very little about the "official" contact, so an earlier one can be described in any way. But we already know what happened in the first human-Romulan contact. In fact, we know very well: "Balance of Terror" is considered one of Star Trek's finest episodes, and it was made very clear that it was the Federation's first contact since the wars of one hundred years before. To suggest it happened differently, with James Kirk's father on his ship, is just too unbelievable. And the fact that George Kirk never told his son what happened, even if it was supposed to be classified, is even more unbelievable.

Unfortunately, the parts of the story involving Jim Kirk do not work too well, either. While rereading his father's letters one sunny afternoon, Kirk begins to feel he is missing something and that he does not want to live the life his father led. He actually decides to give up command of the *Enterprise*. McCoy shows up and tries to talk him out of it, and even Spock makes an appearance before the end of the story. The way *Final Frontier* is set up, Kirk's reflections are interspersed among sections involving the story with Kirk's father. The reader must read through several chapters of George Kirk's adventure before James Kirk's decision is revealed. It is not a surprise when we learn he will not be leaving the *Enterprise* after all. Ironically, the writing in this section is very good. Ms. Carey seemed to capture Kirk's grief after losing Edith Keeler and his feeling that he is missing out on certain things in life.

The section of the story dealing with Kirk's father is also well written. George Samuel Kirk is a very likable character, as are Robert April, Dr. Sarah Poole (later April's wife), and George's fellow officer and friend, Drake Reed. We see George Kirk's pain at being away from his two young sons. Robert April, a peaceful man at heart, realizes that sometimes might makes right. However, while written very well, there are just too many flaws in *Final Frontier* for it to be that enjoyable. The Romulan commander who George saves ends up saving the humans; he is tired of his own race's shortsightedness, much as the Romulan commander in "Balance of Terror" is tired of the constant Romulan need for military conflict. There is also a battle scene in *Frontier* that is very similar to the final battle scene in *Wrath of Khan*, when Kirk tells Scotty he needs power in two minutes or "we're all dead."

Taken on its own, *Final Frontier* may have been a good story, but it is just too similar to *Strangers* and, in some ways, this detracts from the enjoyment of both books. Both stories use James Kirk as the central figure to tell the main story, both with the use of flashbacks and Kirk going through a period of adjustment in his life. Both stories only use Kirk, Spock, and McCoy as opposed to the entire crew of regulars. Both tell the story of a first contact taking place before what we have been previously told is the official one. And, finally, both are similarly divided into sections, with the events of the past and the current story setting interspersed with each other, most probably to heighten the tension.

Flashbacks are tricky things. It is very difficult to put characters in dangerous situations and keep tension when the reader knows that the character is not going to die or be changed in any significant way. In *Strangers*, we know the members of the landing party are not going to die, even though they are placed in life-threatening situations. And the use of a flashback in *Frontier* to prolong the suspense as to whether or not Kirk will relinquish command of the *Enterprise* is pointless; James Kirk has always returned to the *Enterprise* after losing a woman.

Based on these similarities, the fact that *Final Frontier* was published as a giant Star Trek novel right after *Strangers From the Sky* is very surprising. While I realize that these projects were probably in development at the same time, I just hope the next giant Star Trek novel won't be about how Spock's father found a Horta on a planet ten years before "Devil in the Dark" and the story unfolds as Amanda remembers the time she almost lost her husband. In all seriousness, I hope we have seen the last plot concerning a first contact before the official one, set in a flashback, for quite some time.

In conclusion, *Enterprise, Strangers From the Sky*, and *The Final Frontier* are not bad Star Trek novels, though *Frontier* has few redeeming qualities. My point is simply that if these giant Star Trek novels are going to be portrayed as something different or extra special, then that is what the reader should receive. And except for *Strangers*, which has only a few flaws, *Enterprise* and *Frontier* are not stories that I would consider to be different or special.

Actually, I am curious about the plot of the next giant Star Trek novel. The current theme seems to be major events in a character's life—in these cases, Kirk's. I would not be surprised to see giant stories about the years between the end of the television series and the time of *Star Trek: The Motion Picture* (a story idea currently under development by J. M. Dillard), Kirk's early years at the Academy, or events early in his career or even some major event before or after a time that would include the *Enterprise* regulars. The good news is that we can still look forward to the "regular" Star Trek novel, because it may be just as good, or even better, than a "giant" Star Trek novel.

A CRITIQUE
OF SPOCK'S WORLD

by Lou E. Mason

I took up Diane Duane's Star Trek novel *Spock's World* with great anticipation. Here, the back of the jacket promised, Spock would reveal the secrets of Vulcan, which "have lain hidden beneath its burning sands." There was trepidation as well, however, because I had read Duane's *The Romulan Way* and so was familiar with her ideas on the origin of the Romulans/Rihannsu and also with the direction which her concept of Vulcan mind-skills had taken since her earlier book, *My Enemy, My Ally*.

But as I read *Spock's World*, the anticipation faded and unease grew. In view of the great success which is being claimed for this book, I felt I would like to share with the readers of *Trek* my concerns about this novel, which I fear will bring future speculation about the subjects it touches to a dead end.

It seems to me that there are many problems with *Spock's World*. They can be divided into four main categories:

Content
- credibility of the plot
- discrepancies with the rest of Star Trek

• internal inconsistencies

Characterization and use of language

I will discuss the problems with plot plausibility first, since it is crucial to any fiction, but perhaps most of all to science fiction, that the author be able to convince her readers that her imaginary world is real. In science fiction, suspension of disbelief depends in large part on the author's control of and respect for current scientific knowledge and theory. That does not mean she must adhere to it slavishly; if she did, she might be writing fiction but it would not be science fiction. The author must base her universe on science, and must then speculate in a logical and coherent way about how that science and technology could develop under the circumstances she is postulating. There are several plot elements in *Spock's World* which are difficult to believe, because they contravene current scientific knowledge. While none of them is essential to the plot, taken together they weaken the fabric of the whole. I will not attempt a comprehensive list, but will mention only those which I felt to be most distracting.

In "Vulcan One," Duane refers to the primordial soup of Vulcan as producing "Vulcan analogues of DNA and RNA." As we all know, these are the nucleic acids which carry the genetic information and (in higher organisms) transcribe it into the proteins which carry out all the various cellular functions of life. (Some viruses have only RNA, which serves both functions for them.) There has been much speculation in Star Trek criticism as to how two species as dissimilar as human and Vulcan, with their anatomical differences, the different oxygen-binding metals in their blood, the different balance of salts in their intracellular and presumably their extracellular fluids—all documented in the original series—could have been hybridized to produce a functional life form. Now Diane Duane tells us that in addition to these barriers to interbreeding, the two species are faced with "analogues" in the very molecules which determine inheritance: the DNA and RNA of human and and Vulcans are not the same. It staggers the imagination that these two species could be hybridized successfully, even by the genius of the Vulcan Science Academy. Later, in "Vulcan Seven," we are told that ATP/AMP "systems" are also different in the two life forms. That is consistent with the dissimilar DNA/RNA, but it is not consistent with successful hybridization, since the ATP/ADP/AMP enzymes are essential sources of energy for such fundamental intracellular functions as metabolism of glucose and synthesis of proteins. In fact, Duane states, "even the basic bodily cell structure . . . from the mitochondria up" are incompatible. On Earth, basic cellular structure and physiology are universal, but still we cannot fuse even two life forms so close as dogs and cats. If every aspect of life, from the genetic building blocks to the enzymes they code for, to the structures of the cells they build, are incompatible between the two species, how in the name of logic can anyone believe they can be combined into a single, functioning organism?

Our credulity is stretched even further when Duane states that the interspecies pregnancy, once achieved, came to term without incident. What about the adverse effects on mother and embryo/fetus of the exchange across the placenta of one's iron and sodium for the other's copper and potassium (or other cation —we are never told what Spock has instead of sodium that the salt vampire finds distasteful)? As anyone with knowledge of animal physiology is aware, iron, copper, sodium, and other cations are kept in a delicate balance in the body, and excess or deficiency of any can cause serious illness or even death. But the placenta is permeable to these ions; if their concentrations differ in fluids on either side, they will cross the placenta until the concentrations equilibrate. And what about the immune response of the human mother to her half-Vulcan embryo? How can that be suppressed so that the mother's body does not reject the embryo as the body tries to reject anything it recognizes as foreign—a transplanted heart, bacteria, cancer cells, one's mate's sperm, one's own sperm?

In "Enterprise Eight," we see T'Pau dying, Duane says, of liver failure. T'Pau is green, we are told. It is true that humans develop a somewhat greenish tinge when their livers fail, although it is usually described as yellow (jaundice). This is due to the color of the degradation product of iron-based hemoglobin, bilirubin, which accumulates in the body when the liver cannot clear it. Since Vulcan blood is based on copper, not bilirubin, it is unlikely that liver failure in a Vulcan would color her green.

The same problem with copper occurs earlier in the book, when the oceans are described as "green as old bronze." Presumably, bronze on Vulcan is the same as bronze on Earth and does not change from its unoxidized reddish-orange color to its oxidated green unless it is, in fact, oxidized. On Earth, at least, that does not occur in water, but only upon exposure to damp air.

The existence or nonexistence of a natural Vulcan satellite is another problem. In this Duane is caught, like all Star Trek writers since the release of *Star Trek: The Motion Picture*, between what Spock tells Uhura in "The Enemy Within" ("Vulcan has no moon") and what we see hanging over Vulcan, obscuring more than a third of its night sky, on the Heights of Gol. Duane tries to resolve this discrepancy by saying, as Jean Lorrah did before her in *The Vulcan Academy Murders*, that this is a binary planet, T'Khut, not a true moon. (Lorrah called Vulcan's sister T'Kuht.) The problem with that explanation is that a planet so massive and so close to Vulcan would wreak all sorts of havoc on Vulcan's atmosphere and tectonics—as Vulcan would on T'Khut's. As inhospitable as Vulcan is, the planet which would result from the presence of such an enormous binary planet so close would make what we know of Spock's world seem like a veritable paradise in comparison. I think the only logical thing to do with the monster we see in *STTMP* is to ignore it. (In my family, many theories have been advanced to explain it, including Vulcan Space Central hanging low to watch Spock fail Kolinahr, a gigantic hot-air balloon, or a sperm whale deposited by the infinite-probability drive described in Douglas Adams' *Hitchhiker's Guide to the Galaxy*. All of them seem as probable as T'Khut.)

To switch from astronomy to anthropology, Duane presents us with a perplexing problem in her otherwise very appealing portrait of primeval Vulcans. Here we have a loose collection of gatherers who have not yet developed speech. Their telepathic communication is limited to "halting picture-speech . . . incomplete, fragmentary." They do, however, have the capacity for symbolic thought. They can question why one would want to bother carrying water when there is always enough, when water is heavy. "What was the point?" They can conceptualize God. These concepts are quite obviously beyond a mind which cannot understand symbols.

Finally, there is a very basic and very distressing discrepancy in Duane's vision of a pre-Reformation Vulcan armed with weapons capable of annihilation of all life on a planet. Duane's historical Vulcan has nuclear weapons, "dirty" and "clean," and they are used in the continuous tribal wars; but nevertheless, miraculously—or as Diane Duane puts it, "for some reason"—life is not annihilated. Vulcan has matter/antimatter weapons and has used them on the outer planets (presumably of Vulcan's solar system), on the colonies, and eventually on T'Khut, but Vulcan survives. We see this same naive view of nuclear war in Duane's description of Earth, which is still fighting wars with post-atomic weapons as late as 2162. But our twentieth-century science teaches us that nuclear war is incompatible with life. Duane's description of war in an atomic age and after as minor, her premise that a civilization could survive centuries of nuclear war (in Earth's case) or millennia (in Vulcan's), obviates one of Star Trek's most vital lessons for our time: War is suicide.

In addition to these errors in science, Duane commits a number of mistakes which are even more detrimental to the success of *Spock's World*. These are discrepancies, some quite major, others minor and of only nuisance value, with the rest of Star Trek lore. To me, these discrepancies are more upsetting than the errors in science. After all, every Trek fan knows that scientific accuracy is not Star Trek's long suit. We are willing to overlook certain blunders for the sake of enjoying our favorite characters interacting with each other and with their universe. But one thing we do insist on: that our favorite characters and their universe be at least moderately consistent within the framework set up for them. We do not insist on total agreement; within the corpus of Star Trek itself there are many discrepancies. The original series is rife with them, the animated episodes continue the tradition, the novels enlarge it considerably, and the movies, eventually, have honored it as well. Most of them do not bother us; we accept them as differences in vision between their creators. At worst, they annoy us. At best, they provide us with a wide variety of ideas and the chance to debate them among ourselves in private or here, in the pages *Best of Trek*. But when an episode ("The Cloud Minders" is a notorious example), an animated story ("The Lorelei Signal" and "The Terratin Incident," with their use of the transporter to solve the crises), or a novel such as *Spock's World* creates conflicts with the established fundamentals of Star Trek, we are upset, and justifiably so.

And eight of the primary assumptions of *Spock's World* are in direct conflict with the rest of Star Trek.

First, we have the problem of the Vulcan mind skills. On this question Duane herself changed position between her earlier novel *My Enemy, My Ally* and her later ones, *The Romulan Way* and *Spock's*

World. Initially she described them much as we see in the series: touch telepathy. The Rihannsu are attempting to steal back the skills they have lost by cloning Vulcan genetic material, but they are hoping to learn also how to enhance the mind skills to the level of true telepathy and mind control. It is clear that the Vulcans in *My Enemy, My Ally* do not have these mental powers. By the time she wrote *The Romulan Way,* however, Duane seemed to have learned something about Vulcans that no one else knows: Now Vulcans are true telepaths. They have mind-trees. (In *Spock's World* these telepathic "grapevines" can traverse interstellar space and are used as some humans today use narcotics, for escape from humdrum existence.) They can drive and guide starships with psionic power. They can attack and tear up the spaceships of the invading Duthuliv pirates. In *Spock's World* Duane develops the precept of mind-skills even further: Vulcans can force their way into one another's minds telepathically and steal secrets. They can control each other with telepathy. They can "beam images of destruction back" to the pirates' home planets over interstellar distances. They can, and do, kill.

There are two problems with this concept of Vulcan mind power. First, there is no evidence of such extensive powers in the original series, the animated series, or the films. All we see is touch-telepathy and a hint (in "The Immunity Syndrome" and "The Devil in the Dark," for example) of covert true telepathy. Second, powers of that degree would make Vulcans invincible. And we know for certain that Vulcans are not invincible. If they were, there would be no problems for the

Enterprise crew to solve. There would be no dramatic tension. There would be no Star Trek.

The second primary assumption of *Spock's World* which I find unacceptable is the exodus of the dissidents who would eventually become the Rihannsu. Duane repeats in this novel her premise formulated in *The Romulan Way* that eighty thousand Vulcans who were unhappy with the newly emerging Reformed Society of Surak left the planet on spaceships which took years and a cooperative effort in terms of planning, engineering, and financing to build. As mentioned above, mind-skills were an essential part of the drives and guidance of these vessels.

Why does this beggar belief? First, because I cannot conceive of a culture advanced enough to have space flight and with mindadepts powerful enough to drive and guide starships launching a whole armada of ships into space and then . . . losing them. Despite all the mind-skills, despite the tracking devices necessary for space flight on that scale, those ships just disappeared. No one knows when the Rihannsu reappear centuries later to attack the infant Federation who they are or where they came from. The Rihannsu themselves do not know.

In *The Romulan Way* Duane makes an attempt to explain this, but her explanation does not ring true. It seems that the mindadepts died out—because of overuse of their powers in "bootstrapping" their ships, because of disease—and that none were left to train new ones who had the inherent ability. But Duane does not explain how Vulcans would permit themselves to get to the point of no return with their psitechs. Surely, if a certain minimum number was

131

necessary to perpetuate the more advanced skills they would have known that and would not have risked that core until others could be trained. And surely there would have been new ones: The genetic trait for mind-skills logically cannot be an all-or-nothing proposition. That would require a single gene, or perhaps multiple genes with a single enabling gene—a highly unlikely genetic arrangement for so complex and variable a set of powers. If there were survivors with any degree of mind-skills, it should have been possible to breed for those traits. It should, one would think, have been given the highest priority, especially in view of the fact that Duane tells us in *Spock's World* that eugenics was the method used to develop the psionic powers to the extraordinary degree they had reached by Surak's day. And surely some inherent skills must be available without complex training, or how would the mind-skills have arisen in the first place? Duane also fails to explain how all the mind-adepts left on Vulcan could have lost track of the Travelers who, despite the many hazards of their long journey, were still eighteen thousand strong at starfall.

Second, if the Rihannsu left Vulcan that recently, how did they happen to lose their mind-skills? We know from "All Our Yesterdays" that Spock's ancestors were barbarians five thousand years ago, and no matter what type of year he means—Vulcan year, solar year, or Sarpeidon year—that is very little time for so major a change to occur. In terms of a culture whose calendar dates at that time in six figures, the middle of the 139,900s, it is a drop in the bucket. In evolutionary terms, it's a drop in the ocean. As discussed above, Duane's claims that all the trained mind-

132

adepts among the Travelers burned themselves out and left only untrained (and untrainable novices) seems a little too facile, and does not answer why the logical Vulcans would permit this or why a new generation could not have begun relearning the mind-skills from the ground up. It is, I feel, a plot device foisted upon the reader because the author could not be bothered to find a consistent method to reach her desired goal.

A related problem arises from the timing of the development of starflight capability. Diane Duane puts this relatively early in Vulcan history; that is, before the advent of Surak and his Reformed Society. Vulcans, as we know from Spock, were on the verge of annihilating themselves when Surak came onto the scene and saved the day with logic and the control of emotion. War was a way of life with them, as well as probably the most common cause of death. But if they had spaceships before Surak, whey did they not arm those spaceships and conquer every civilization within reach? Why would they be content just to squabble among themselves for Vulcan's admittedly meager resources?

According to Duane ("Vulcan Five"); "Military [ships], oddly enough, had not yet been conceived of." Oddly enough is right! Duane intimates that this is related to the lack of a standing army, but someone has to be fighting all those recurrent wars, and someone has to be manning the merchant space marines. It does seem a little astonishing that the brilliant and war-loving Vulcans would not have thought of arming spaceships and rampaging over the galaxy. However, Duane contradicts herself later: In "Vulcan Six" we are told that Vulcan has used matter/antimatter weapons on the outer planets and space colonies. *That* sounds more like the pre-Reformation Vulcan we know and love to tremble at!

That brings me to my next concern: the character of Vulcan society before the Reformation of Surak. Duane presents us in *Spock's World* with a series of vignettes of life on Vulcan at different periods. The earlier ones, with certain reservations such as the extent of Vulcan mind-skills, the use of nuclear weapons in the numerous, protracted wars, etc., are fairly plausible. As she approaches the time of Surak, however, what she describes is an increasingly Earth-like society. Surak lives in a world of offices. He works late at the computer to produce business reports, half aware of broadcast news on what is essentially television. Life on Vulcan is petty and mundane. It is all very familiar—too familiar, in fact. Apart from the Vulcan mind-skills and their use against business rivals, and the names of the principalities and kingdoms which are at war with each other, it could be twentieth-century Earth.

Worse, the Vulcans themselves have no qualities which distinguish them from humans. Throughout Vulcan history, as Duane describes it, no one on Vulcan displays any concept of loyalty or honor or any other of the ethical beliefs which are essential to a civilization, or even to a loose association of gatherers.

At best we see pragmatism—doing what is best for the group because it is best for "me"—and the self-preserving kind of loyalty which exists between mates. Even in Surak's time these are lacking. Surak himself is not particularly distressed by the endless reports on the news of betrayal, the forcing of one sentient mind by another, murder, war after war. There is nothing in this Vulcan society for Surak to build his Reformed Society on, no basic decency or concern for others to foretell that life and the inviolability of the sentient mind will become sacrosanct.

Where did these ethics spring from, then, in Diane Duane's opinion? Did Surak create them from whole cloth and in some way convert all of voracious, violent, unprincipled Vulcans to them? Even if he were a rhetorician of the most sublime or satanic demagogic gifts, he would not be able to accomplish that. A person or a society can only develop along the path made accessible to it by its inherent gifts. We cannot take an average person and turn him into an Einstein, a Gandhi, a Bach, simply by haranguing him about physics, peace, or music. Even a writer as articulate and moving as Shakespeare could not accomplish that, and the samples of Surak's writings which Duane provides for us do not exhibit any extraordinary eloquence. They are initially chatty, later precious, finally sermonizing, and always emotional. I have trouble believing they would convince anyone of anything, but then I have never found television evangelists particularly persuasive, either, and that is the style Duane ascribes to Surak.

That raises another point about Surak which is inconsistent with the rest of Star Trek. We see Surak—or Spock's concept of Surak, which I think we can accept as reasonably accurate—only once, in "The Savage Curtain." He is so unemotional that he comments even on Spock's surprise at seeing him. But the Surak Diane Duane shows us in *Spock's World* speaks and writes and reacts emotionally. His transcendental experience with the "Underlier" is one initially of fear, then of joy. No logic or mastery of emotion was involved. His early philosophy is one of love, expressed with exclamation points and italics. There is no explanation how, when or why this changed to one of logic and non-emotion.

Perhaps that is the reason we do not see any real growth in the modern Vulcans of *Spock's World*. Surak's philosophy might have removed war from their world, but all the individual vices which promote war remain. A distressing—even shocking—number of Duane's citizens of the Reformed Society are driven by the same motivations and emotions as their barbarian ancestors were, and as we are: anger, fear, jealousy, hurt pride, lust, greed, prejudice. They can be bribed, fooled by demagogues and propaganda, they have no curiosity to discover the truth for themselves. Vulcans without curiosity? Even Duane's primordial Vulcan the Wanderer was driven by his Vulcan curiosity. Vulcans, T'Pring says in a cynical description which sounds very much like an Earth politician speaking about his constituency in private—but which Duane confirms by her plot—"will say things that they hear others say, whether they truly believe them or not. And if they say them often enough, they will come to believe them anyway." This bodes ill for Vulcan. It casts doubt on the viability of its society, whether it stays in the Federation or not. It also eradicates the entire reason for the existence of Vulcan in the Star Trek universe: Vulcan is merely another Earth, Vulcans just another race of humans, one whose ears happen to be pointed and whose blood happens to be green. What is the point of infinite diversity in infinite combinations if all it can achieve is humans with green blood and pointed ears?

Finally, we come to the question of *pon farr*. This feature of "Vulcan biology" has always fascinated Star Trek fans, female fans especially perhaps. Oddly, Duane does not seem to have developed a consistent idea about it. We see it in *Spock's World* from the earliest humanoids on Vulcan onward, in the gatherers described in "Vulcan Two," so we know (if "Amok Time" and *The Search for Spock* had left any doubt) that it is biologically and not culturally determined. Yet its overriding power is not evident in this novel, not at any point in Vulcan history. Mahak, in "Vulcan Four" is "past the Raptures without ill effect," but unbonded. Despite the seven-year cycle, Nomikh in "Vulcan Five" has survived forty years as a widower. Unless he has been committing incest or availing himself of his sons' wives, this would seem to contradict Spock's statement that a Vulcan must take a wife or die in *pon farr*.

Sarek has been spared the inconvenience of *pon farr* as well, apparently, at least until he was considerably older than the approximately thirty-six Vulcan years we know Spock was when he was first stricken. Sarek, according to Duane, left Vulcan as a young adult, remained on Earth "more than fifty years" without mating, as far as we can tell, went back to Vulcan still unbonded, and did not marry Amanda until some unspecified time after his return to Earth as the Vulcan ambassador.

Spock, also seems to have been spared further episodes of *pon farr*. Since Kirk is presented in *Spock's World* as an admiral demoted to captain, the events

137

must take place well after the series and probably after *The Voyage Home*. We know from *Wrath of Khan* that some fifteen years passed between the first year of the series and the second Star Trek movie, so Spock should have had at least two recurrences of the Time of Mating. Yet he appears to be unbonded. I doubt that Kirk would have volunteered to undergo combat with him again for the sake of their friendship, and certainly Spock would not have accepted his offer if he had. A mystery, or just the author ignoring a question which would complicate or nullify some of her plot devices?

Before I go on to the more minor discrepancies in *Spock's World*, I would like to voice my concerns about the Underlier.

Duane uses her version of Shi-hulud to reinforce the mysticism of the Wanderer's experience at Mount Seleya and of Surak's with his vision of apocalypse. To me this is not only unnecessary but artistically dishonest. The experiences should stand on their own merits if they are well conceived and well written. The Underlier is also hinted at as the source of some of Surak's persuasiveness, as if "another presence [were] encouraging them" to make peace. Again, a cheat: Surak's philosophy should also stand on its own merits. The Father of All We Have Become should not need the help of a sand god.

There are numerous less serious inconsistencies with accepted facts documented in other parts of the Star Trek corpus. There is, for example, the question of dates. We know from the bottle of Romulan ale in *The Wrath of Khan* (stamped 2283) that we are near the end of the twenty-third century by that time. (There has been considerable debate, some here in *Best of Trek*, about why a contraband liquor which has to be smuggled across the Neutral Zone would be labeled in Federation Standard and have a Terran date, but since it has never been resolved, I think we will have to accept that date as correct.) But Diane Duane claims that the first encounter between Vulcans and humans occurred in 2065, and Spock says (on page 37) that 156 years have passed since then. That places this story in 2221.

Another problem with dates arises in "Vulcan Seven." Sarek goes to Earth before 2162, returns in 2212 (unmarried), and meets Amanda soon afterward. Their courtship follows for an unspecified time, and more time passes before he and Amanda go to Vulcan to seek the help of the Vulcan Science Academy in having a child. The geneticists work on the project for four years, and the pregnancy itself requires nine and a half months (Lunar? T'Khutian?) to come to term. Therefore, Spock cannot have been born before 2220. So how can this be 2221? Another dating problem: Kirk tells the debate that Vulcan joined the Federation 180 years ago, although Spock says the first encounter was 156 years ago. These two are, of course, internal inconsistencies as well as conflicts with another facet of Star Trek, the sort of carelessness which detracts immeasurably from any work of fiction. But more about that later.

We also have discrepancies in technology. In the prologue we learn the *Enterprise* is provisioned with real food, textiles, etc. In the series the computer-operated synthesizers create food and presumably clothing, or at least the costumes the landing parties wear when it would be inappropriate for them to wear their Starfleet uniforms. (Later in the same chapter, however, the computer is making meatloaf—another internal inconsistency.

Surak drives a car which uses fuel, not, as would be logical on Vulcan, solar power. Earth in the early twenty-third century is still using vehicles with internal combustion engines, Fahrenheit thermometers, and foot-pound measurements—irrational systems which hopefully we will be able to abandon by the end of this century.

Vulcan is said to be twelve light-years from Earth, which at warp two according to the usually accepted formula (warp $n = n^3$ c) would take 547.5 Earth days, not "a little less than two," as Duane states in "Enterprise One." It might have been better if Kirk had ordered warp eight, which would have taken only 8.55 days according to this formula, since there seemed to be some urgency involved in the mission.

Vulcans have not developed a method of harnessing the heat of their sun, and so must comply with the custom of siesta which we have here on Earth in hot climates. It is difficult to imagine a culture less compatible with the siesta life-style.

There are also incompatibilities with Vulcan culture as it is presented elsewhere in Star Trek, or as we can safely deduce from what we do see. Apart from the major problems discussed above, we have the matter of the preliminary bonding of children. Diane Duane has T'Pau state that this is elective in her family; so why did Sarek have Spock bonded to T'Pring?

KhasWan is a puzzle as well. In the prologue Sarek remembers his maturity ordeal with the catchphrase,

"At the day's end he would either be a man or be dead." A man? At age seven?

We also see Sarek sent to Earth as essentially a computer technician, with the unofficial duty of serving as liaison to T'Pau, who apparently does not trust the ambassador's reports. Sarek never has any training in diplomacy, but he is promoted to a public-relations officer-travel agent, then to a diplomatic post, apparently because of his familiarity with Earth and his fluency in its languages. Eventually he is appointed ambassador, still with no formal training. This seems strange for a man who was so insistent on his son's staying to study formally at the Vulcan Science Academy that it caused a deep rift between them for eighteen years. It also seems uncharacteristic of a society as exacting and as devoted to form as is Vulcan's.

The last type of conflict with other sources of Star Trek I would like to mention is the confusion, which Diane Duane only increases, of what Vulcan is like. In "Amok Time," we see a red sky. In *The Search for Spock* and *The Voyage Home*, the sky varies from red to pinkish beige. We have to accept the fact, however, that while the scene painters for the series could color the Vulcan sky whatever tint the creators wanted, the cameramen for the movies probably did not shoot the Vulcan scenes on Vulcan. We do see in the movies Vulcan's red sand, and Mt. Seleya is very rust-colored. In *Spock's World*, for some reason, the sky of Vulcan is the blue-white of Earth, and the sand and Mt. Seleya are white. And the stars look the same from Vulcan as they do from Earth, despite the difference in position, the difference in viewpoint, and the very marked difference in atmosphere.

Now to the strictly internal inconsistencies. Some of these I have mentioned above. The others, on the whole, are relatively unimportant. They are also careless and unnecessary. And they do detract from the credibility of the novel, or to borrow one of Duane's Surak's favorites, they increase its entropy.

We learn in "Vulcan Two" that primeval Vulcans do not laugh and are ambivalent about emotions, but we see no such reluctance or ambivalence in later Vulcans. Even Sarek is portrayed as laughing. Surely, as Spock tells us in the series, it is not that modern Vulcans are lacking emotions or even that their ancestors were ambivalent about them. Their passions were too strong, too overwhelming. It was their "animal passions," as the Master of Gol puts it, which led them to the brink of self-destruction. They overcame them only by continual personal and societal struggle. To ascribe to a stone-age people ambivalence about emotion and suppression of laughter is to diminish the magnitude of that struggle. It is to write Vulcan small.

In "Vulcan Three" we are told that the clan of the Eye is south of Phelsh't, but when they migrate southwest, the butte appears on their left.

In "Enterprise One" the bulletin-board system is dated Stardate 7412.17. Stardates are difficult to interpret. In the series a single digit seemed to represent a ship's day. My theory about their chronology is that they change from sector to sector, with zero for each sector being determined by when the first Earth ship explored it, Starfleet being the geocentric organization it is. However, Earth and Vulcan should be in the same sector, so there would be no reason for the stardates to jump two hundred numbers to 7611 in

"Enterprise Four," in what Duane says is "less than two days."

McCoy solves T'Pring's part in the debates by wondering how she could have amassed so much money "without being noticed." This is Vulcan, Bones, with Vulcan rules of privacy in full force: Who would ask? And how would he know how much she inherited from Stonn?

Sarek says in "Vulcan Seven" that he is "nearly the youngest of his House." Are there no children? This kind of statement adds nothing, and would add nothing even if it were accurate, except that one would have to worry about the survival of the House of Surak.

Vulcan has, as we all know, no moon, but Duane and even her Vulcan characters refer to T'Khut as a moon and the length of its cycle as a month. Granted, in "Yesteryear," Spock himself refers to the month of Tasmeen, but it is probably a simple mistranslation for a more rational Vulcan division of the year. When the two Spocks are out on the L'laglon mountains at night, there is no moon to light the darkness for them, yet in *Spock's World* T'Khut's presence seems inescapable.

Finally in the category of internal inconsistencies, there are simple errors of grammar, usage, logic, arithmetic. These are not major, just a sign of carelessness, so I will not bore us with a complete list. But such statements as "When cause does not necessarily follow effect" can only detract, bit by bit, from the whole.

Kroyka. Enough of that nit-picking and on to something far more significant: the poverty of interpersonal relationships and the faulty characterization from which it arises. In *Spock's World*, the most flourishing relationship seems to be between the recreation computer and her boss, Chief of Recreation Harb Tanzer. Between Spock, Kirk, and McCoy there is some teasing and some joking, but even in a situation as potentially devastating for Spock as having his two parental worlds estranged, of having to make a choice of one or the other, or perhaps not even being given that choice, perhaps even being cast out of Vulcan society as an impure half-breed, there is very little of Kirk offering his friend support or understanding. This is the sort of defect which many fans feel spoiled *Star Trek: The Motion Picture*, and which one would hope a Star Trek novel would have grown beyond. In the historical vignettes, Diane Duane shows she can handle relationships, but her hand is less sure with the characters for whom most of us read and watch Star Trek: Kirk, Spock, McCoy, and the bridge crew. For some reason she seems to have lost the deft touch with characterization which she had in *My Enemy, My Ally*, especially with Kirk and Spock and the unique relationship between them. In *Spock's World*, Duane's failure to comprehend these central figures of Star Trek shows also in her inability to differentiate them by giving them distinctive styles of speaking or thinking. They all speak and they all think alike.

In the prologue, Duane depicts Spock sitting on the bridge of the *Enterprise*, amusing himself with idle speculation about others' feelings, a pastime which seems singularly out of character. When Spock briefs the senior officers about the situation on Vulcan, he speaks in a graceless mixture of formal and colloquial English: "The groups who want us out for fear of Vulcan being contaminated are in the ascendant in numbers and popularity." He says, "I am afraid"—an adjective with marked emotional overtones which a Vulcan would not use casually—when he means, "I regret." He estimates "odds" with uncharacteristic imprecision as "on the close order of seventy percent"—which is not an expression of odds at all. Before all of Vulcan he avers that he holds *cthia* "dear."

Jim Kirk is even more poorly characterized. Even after all these years he still thinks that Spock's ears are the wrong shape. When addressing a Vulcan audience in the Hall of Voices he patronizes them by calling them "you people" and insults their Explorers by ascribing to them delight and boredom, neither of which would be acceptable to modern Vulcans. (The modern Vulcans in *Spock's World* do not seem to notice, however—they should.) He makes racist jokes about Vulcan ears and Spock's hybrid genetics which, incredibly, the Vulcans laugh at. As mentioned before, he shows none of the special care and love for Spock which we know he feels toward his old and peculiarly vulnerable friend. He defends him against a sneer at his half-Vulcan genetics in public, but he seems to have nothing to spare for him in private.

Others fare no better. T'Pau "desires" a result and steps down from her formal pedestal to call Kirk "James." She describes Terrans as "charming." Although Spock once said that a Vulcan would not cry out under torture ("The Savage Curtain"), the Vulcan whom K's't'lk nips on the leg cries out "with great enthusiasm," as the artful glass spider triumphantly notes. The other Vulcans in the audience at the debate call questions from the floor in idiomatic language and laugh—even at inanities or at insults which should offend them. I found this "canned laughter" no less annoying in *Spock's World* than I do when one of my children subjects me to a sitcom on television. After all, it does serve the same function: to inform the ignorant audience that they have just heard a funny joke.

Perhaps worst served of all the characters in *Spock's World* is Sarek. He comes across in the book as a very different man from the Sarek we see in "Journey to Babel," "Yesteryear," *The Search for Spock*, and *The Voyage Home*.

Diane Duane's Sarek has a sense of humor. He is unkempt and tends to throw his dirty laundry about. On the verge of his journey to Earth he feels homesick before he has even left Vulcan. He has trouble adjusting his Vulcan brain to the old systems of measurement with which Duane anachronistically saddles twenty-second-century Terra. He admires human computer technicians not for their skill but for their love of their craft. He enjoys learning about things Terran, including fish soup—certainly forbidden to Vulcans. He studies language happily and mimics regional accents to get a laugh. He smiles freely, speaks idiomatically and with exclamation points, and is described as having an uncontrollable fit of laughter in response to a not very amusing insult. He uses his Vulcan mind-skills in negotiations, and it does not seem to matter whether he has the consent of his adversaries. His relationship with his predecessor in the Vulcan Embassy is described initially as one of "worship" and subsequently as "warm and cordial," neither of which is appropriate to a man of pure logic. His use of language is, like Spock's, impossible to distinguish from that of anyone else: He says "I fear" instead of "I regret," he uses words imprecisely ("an emotion so crass and debasing as blame"—blame is not an emotion, but an assessment of causality, which may be perfectly logical). He calls Kirk "Jim." In the formal debate in the Hall of Voices, he tells the audience that he will "speak as I *feel* (italics mine) I must speak" and he uses clumsy and ungrammatical language: ". . . against which it lacks the data . . . to have any resistance to, to begin with . . ."

Although he has lived on Earth for eighty-odd years by the time the story takes place and has become so expert in the customs and languages of Earth that he is promoted from computer technician to ambassador, in spite of his lack of formal training in diplomacy, somehow in all those years and with all his Vulcan curiosity, he has managed to remain ignorant of the significance of pointed ears in Terran demonology. It seems an inexplicable oversight, and Duane does not explain it. This is another unfortunate use of an unexamined plot device for the sake of its effect. Sarek's courtship of Amanda Grayson appears to be only a little less precipitous than a human's might be. Its consummation—before marriage, an event which must be (with the possible exception of T'Pring and Stonn) unique in modern Vulcan society—is described coyly as an extension of their discussion of the meaning of the Vulcan word *arie'mnu.* Furthermore, he considers this a suitable topic about which to tease her, in public. Vulcan privacy? Vulcan modesty? Vulcan suppression of emotion, especially sexual? What are they?

Thus Diane Duane portrays Sarek as a man of humor and ready emotions. In the series, the animated episode, and the two films in which we see him, however, Sarek is the quintessential Vulcan who adheres doggedly to logic without regard to how it will affect him personally. And dramatically, he *has* to be the quintessential Vulcan. If Sarek were like a human man there would be no point in making him the father of Spock; there would be no contrast with Amanda and no tension. Duane blurs the distinction between Sarek and humans just as she blurs the distinction between all other Vulcans and humans, as she blurs the distinction between Vulcan society and human society and between Vulcan history and human history, the distinction between Vulcan speech and thought and human speech and thought. Just as it is impossible to know without being told who is speaking in *Spock's World*, so it is impossible to know who is acting or thinking or feeling: Vulcan or human. They are too much alike.

The main difficulty with *Spock's World*, however, is not its many and serious faults. It is the danger that Pocket Books, having invested a fair sum of money into printing its first Star Trek hardcover novel and promoting it, will decide that this is to be the gold standard of Vulcan history and Spock's family background the gospel by which all subsequent writings must abide. There must be many fans and many potential writers who have very different concepts of Vulcan and of the scientific, historical, and cultural forces which created Spock and made him the complex and fascinating character we see in the series and beyond. Many of these visions are, no doubt, more internally consistent, more credible in scientific terms, and more in keeping with the rest of Star Trek than are Diane Duane's. It would be a grievous loss to Star Trek if at this late date editorial fiat were to decree all future works must bow to *Spock's World*. This would negate one of the most valuable lessons of Star Trek: That the beauty of the universe, of mankind, and of the human mind does indeed spring from infinite diversity in infinite combinations.

STAR TREK'S THIRD SEASON: A WORTHWHILE MIXTURE OF SUCCESS AND FAILURE

by Gregory Herbek

As stated in Allan Asherman's *Star Trek Compendium*, "Continuity is the raw material of anything." One of the primary arguments derogating Star Trek's third season is its loss of continuity with the program's previous two seasons.

In that final year, characters take on personality traits contrary to those already established in the series, and as a result of this change, they react to situations differently than expected by viewers, given the previously determined standards. The changes are radical enough that ultimately a definite gap between the first two seasons and the last has formed. But given the circumstances of specific stories, how much differently are the characters really acting? More important, are their actions justified in light of those circumstances?

In David Gerrold's *The World of Star Trek*, criticisms are leveled against the third-season episode "For the World Is Hollow and I Have Touched the Sky"—criticisms specifically against the characterization of Doctor McCoy, who is supposedly "so out of character, he really isn't Dr. McCoy at all. He's someone else with the same name."

In the episode, the doctor has contracted a fatal disease. Upon beaming into an asteroid/spaceship, he meets Natira, the priestess of the "planet," who falls in love with him. She essentially asks McCoy to be her husband, and eventually he agrees.

It is hardly out of character for McCoy, a dying man, to choose this option. We know his only marriage to have failed and have seen the tragic end of his relationship with Nancy Crater ("The Man Trap"). There is no reason why he would not want to spend the last year of his life with a beautiful woman who really cares for him and has a true desire to learn more about him.

No matter how well one knows a person, one can never be sure how that person will react when suddenly faced with death. McCoy felt he could best confront his dilemma with a woman. Although some would like to have seen him turn to his friends for support, one can't condemn him for his choice. If any character should be scolded, it is Kirk, who refuses to accept his friend's decision. But, like McCoy's decision, Kirk's reaction is realistic. When one stops thinking of these characters as all-perfect heroes and starts thinking of them as human beings with faults and personal needs, the reality of "uncharacteristic" situations sometimes becomes apparent, and one's feelings toward the characters in those situations are heightened.

In the end, of course, the doctor is miraculously cured and returns to the *Enterprise*. Having regained his life, he remembers where his duty lies and that he cannot stay with Natira. If upon being cured, McCoy had refused to leave her, or had even had second thoughts, his actions *would* have been contrary to his previously established personality traits. Instead, he makes a sacrifice not unlike those of Captain Kirk on "City on the Edge of Forever" and Mr. Spock in "This Side of Paradise." All three men, in their respective episodes, have an opportunity to experience true happiness, which none of them have been able to experience before, due to various circumstances. They give up that happiness because of their devotion to duty and each other.

Although instances of seemingly uncharacteristic behavior can sometimes be justified, there are several events and scenes in Star Trek's third season which can be neither explained nor excused.

In "The Cloud Minders," Spock explains the Vulcan mating cycle to Droxine, an acquaintance on the cloud city Stratos. Spock's sexual drive, a subject too personal to discuss with his best friend, Jim Kirk, only a year before in "Amok Time," is relegated to common conversation with a virtual stranger with whom Spock becomes all too intimate. The Vulcan acts similarly uncharacteristically in "The Enterprise Incident." Spock's wooing of the Romulan commander is explainable as a necessary part of his duty, and would be entirely excusable were it not for the final lines:

Spock: All the Federation wanted was the cloaking device.
Commander: The Federation . . . And what did you want?
Spock: It was my only interest . . . when I boarded your vessel.

Commander: And that's exactly what you came away
   with.
Spock: You underestimate yourself, Commander. Military secrets are the most fleeting of all. I hope
   that you and I exchanged something more permanent.

Whereas in the first two seasons, Mr. Spock never
displayed sexually oriented emotions, unless under the
influence of an outside factor, he does so in "The
Cloud Minders" and "The Enterprise Incident," with
nothing to account for the change in his behavior.

Occurrences like these only hastened the general
deterioration of Star Trek, taking place all too often
throughout the third season. The scenes appear, for
the most part, in scripts which are poorly written to
begin with, and are a result of other actions in those
scripts. Therefore, rather than loss of character continuity, the real problem with Star Trek's final season
was its shortage of quality scripts and the abundance
of those less imaginative and sometimes even childish.

Perhaps it was an omen that NBC chose "Spock's
Brain" as the third-season premiere episode. Probably
the worst segment of Star Trek, "Spock's Brain" is
definitely the least imaginative and disregards the importance that Star Trek always placed on believability.

Up through the scene in sickbay, when McCoy informs Kirk that Spock's brain has been removed, the
episode looks to be a promising mystery. From there
the script goes completely downhill, ultimately evolving into little better than a *Space: 1999* episode. Such
poor writing is surprising, at least from Gene L. Coon,

who had provided such fine scripts as "Devil in the Dark" and "Metamorphosis" in the first and second seasons.

Besides supplying generally inferior stories in the third season, Star Trek's writers relied more than ever before on clichés and even reused story lines, as if they were running out of ideas. One of the worst offenders of rehashed plots is "All Our Yesterdays." Although not a poor story in itself, its similarities to "City on the Edge of Forever" are all too apparent. Other, less flagrant examples include "Plato's Stepchildren," which bears some resemblance to "The Gamesters of Triskelion," and "Requiem for Methuselah" and "Whom Gods Destroy," which borrow plot devices from "What Are Little Girls Made of?" and "Dagger of the Mind," respectively. The reuse of previously utilized ideas even took place within the third season itself, as Captain Kirk is missing or presumed dead five times that year alone.

These unnecessary similarities are due either to the laziness of the author or the loss of Gene Roddenberry's guidance in the final season, and in most cases, they could have been avoided with a little imagination.

Although the quality of stories presented in Star Trek's final year deteriorated to a certain degree, Star Trek did not lose itself totally. One of the most important aspects of the show, though not at all its best, was still present throughout the third season—the writers continued to incorporate a moral, sociological, or philosophical message into their scripts. Unfortunately, these messages are sometimes too blatant and/or thinly disguised, and some, although well woven into the scripts, are unsuccessful due to a poor story. This is one reason why Star Trek's final year is the least popular of the series. Unlike most first-season segments, in which all aspects of the episode fit together to produce an overall fine drama, something is too often missing in a third-season script. The story is either ill conceived but contains a fine comment, or vice versa.

"The Cloud Minders," for example, unsuccessfully tackles a serious problem of the sixties—and today—race and class division. In the episode, a world inhabited by two "races" is presented. The "superior" people live in the cloud city Stratos, far above the planet's surface. They engage in intellectual pursuits while the "inferior" race, the Troglytes, work in the caves on Ardana, the harsh planet below. Their inferiority, however, is not inherent, but due rather to an invisible gas natural to the caves in which they live.

The idea of individuals being influenced by their environment was a new theory in the 1960s. A commission appointed by President Lyndon Johnson to examine the race riots late in that decade agreed with the theory and ultimately presented two solutions to race conflict in America: the enrichment of ghetto conditions or the integration of ghetto inhabitants with the rest of society. The latter promised eventual equality for all and the commission supported it; unfortunately, Star Trek did not. "The Cloud Minders" agreed that environment shapes the individual, but did not illustrate the course of action necessary to reverse the widening gap between classes in America. At the episodes' end, the Troglytes are given special masks to filter out the harmful effects of the gas, but are still not allowed to share the benefits of the beautiful cloud city—they continue to live in caves. Whether or not the author's intention, the disheartening statement which the episode ultimately makes is that ghetto conditions can be improved, but those who live there will never join the larger society.

"Turnabout Intruder" suffers from similar problems. The episode blends an interesting concept with a compelling drama, but while exploring the issue of feminism, whether intentionally or not, it conveys a chauvinistic message, contrary to Star Trek's previously established beliefs.

However, for every one of Star Trek's third-season mistakes, there is a triumph. Several of that year's episodes do meet the high standards set by the show's earlier installments.

"Let That Be Your Last Battlefield," despite all complaints of obviousness and blatancy, stands as Star Trek's finest editorial against racial hatred and violence. The issue is brought right out in the open when the *Enterprise* encounters two warring aliens from the planet Cheron. Their faces are divided down the middle, one side black, the other white, the coloration of each side of the face opposite that of the other race.

The parallel to blacks and whites is intentionally unmistakable; the viewer immediately relates the hatred on Cheron to the hatred in America, and therefore does not spend an hour deciphering the episode, but rather continually compares the fictional world it presents with the world he or she lives in. Although this format is inferior to Star Trek's usual disguising of modern-day issues, it works to the advantage of this particular episode.

The aliens, Bele and Lokai, are introduced merely as enemies—the latter and his people supposedly oppressed the former and his people. Not until halfway through the story is it revealed that their different pigmentation is the root of their hostilities—a detail that Kirk and Spock, and the viewer, either do not notice or deem significant until the following discourse:

Bele: It is obvious to the most simpleminded that Lokai is of an inferior breed.

Spock: The obvious visual evidence, Commissioner, is that he is of the same breed as yourself.

Bele: Are you blind, Commander Spock? Well, look at me . . . Look at me.

Kirk: You're black on one side and white on the other.

Bele: I am black on the right side. Lokai is white on the right side. All of his people are white on the right side.

That their intense hatred could be caused by this trivial difference is incomprehensible to Kirk and Spock, who are totally perplexed after the above conversation. Earlier in the episode, when Lokai pleads with Kirk to kill Bele, the captain incredulously says, "You're two of a kind!" As the aliens continue to bicker and battle, the viewer adopts Kirk's attitude of incomprehension and sadness. He or she eventually realizes the absurdity and futility of the aliens' hatred and cannot help but carry at least a little bit of that attitude into the real world.

"Day of the Dove" also deals with war and violence. In this story the crew of the *Enterprise* and that of a Klingon battle cruiser are unknowingly forced to fight by an energy being which lives off the hatred and violence of others. In time Kirk and the Klingon commander realize that their true enemy is not each other, but rather the being which is controlling them. They join together in a successful effort to defeat it by laughing it off the ship.

The human capacity to destroy evil through emotions is a concept also explored in the underrated "And the Children Shall Lead." This episode illustrates how evil misleads the innocent and preys on people's fears to achieve its purpose, and how anyone can defeat it once its true identity and intentions are identified.

"Is There in Truth No Beauty?" is another of the finer segments of Star Trek's last season. A study in human emotions, it deals with jealousy and prejudice. The episode explores Larry Marvick's jealousy, which eventually drives him to attempted murder but, more specifically and importantly, it examines Dr. Miranda Jones' jealousy of Mr. Spock.

For years Miranda, a telepath, has been studying on Vulcan with hopes of becoming the first non-Vulcan to achieve mind meld and, in turn, become the first being to meld with a superior mental race called the Medusans. After Miranda has boarded the *Enterprise* with the Medusan ambassador, with whom she has fallen in love, the ship is plummeted into another dimension. The only way to pilot the ship home is to utilize the ambassador's advanced knowledge of star navigation. Since Medusans have no corporeal form and cannot verbally communicate, the only way to utilize the ambassador's knowledge is by telepathy—the Vulcan mind meld.

Spock is chosen to perform this act rather than Dr. Jones because of his technical knowledge of the *Enterprise*. Unfortunately, by establishing a mind-link with the Medusan, Spock executes the very action which Miranda has devoted her life to achieving. Her dream shattered and her lover's mind, in her opinion, invaded by Spock, she houses intense feelings of jealousy and anger for the Vulcan. With Spock on the brink of death after the meld, the question is whether Miranda, unlike Larry Marvick, will find the courage to overcome her jealousy and aid Spock. She eventually does so and saves the Vulcan's life.

"The Empath" also delves into human emotions, specifically the love that Kirk, Spock, and McCoy feel for one another. In the episode, aliens trap the three officers on a strange planet with plans to use them in a brutal experiment. Also on the planet is a mute empath named Gem, on whose account the experiment is being staged. She is an inhabitant of one of two populated worlds in a doomed star system. Unfortunately, the aliens have the power to save only one of the planets, and are using the men of the *Enterprise* to determine whether Gem's race is the one more worthy of being saved.

They torture Kirk and send him back to Gem, who has the power to alleviate his pain by empathically transferring it to herself. She helps the captain and later risks her life to save McCoy, who has been tortured to the point of death. Gem shows the aliens she has learned compassion, and they judge her planet worthy to be rescued.

Just as each of the men would rather endure the pain than have one of their friends subjected to it,

Gem, who doesn't even know the officers, would rather transfer that pain to herself than watch them suffer.

"The Tholian Web" uses a somewhat clichéd plot device as its focal point—the death of a main character. The problem with this event lies in the viewer's knowledge that a main character in a continuing television series doesn't die, at least not permanently. Therefore, a story which employs this concept must be engaging enough to hold the viewer's attention even though he or she knows the eventual outcome—that the character will be saved or, in this case, will recover. "The Tholian Web" fulfills that requirement and emerges as one of the best episodes of Star Trek's last season.

The apparent death of Captain Kirk kindles some of the finest dramatic interplay between Spock and McCoy in the entire series, revealing much about the Kirk/ Spock/McCoy relationship. Although it was obvious before the events of this episode that Kirk is the stabilizing influence in the friendship, that fact has never been illustrated as clearly as in "The Tholian Web," which reveals the condition of Spock and McCoy's relationship with Kirk (they think) permanently missing from it. Though the doctor truly cares for Spock, without Kirk their friendship would never flourish.

Although other third-season segments, such as "Elaan of Troyius" and "The Savage Curtain" are entertaining, they are not as intellectually stimulating as those cited above or earlier episodes such as "Balance of Terror" and "The Doomsday Machine." So it is true that many third-season installments cannot measure up to Star Trek's earlier accomplishments. But the failures of Star Trek's final year are too often identified and criticized by writers who don't bother to also identify the successes.

In *The World of Star Trek*, David Gerrold writes, "Star Trek's best stories were those that were about people; one or two individuals caught in a trying situation." Miranda Jones, Gem, and Bele and Lokai are such people. They, however, are ignored by Mr. Gerrold. He simply damns the third season and harps upon the excellence of the first, ignoring *its* faults.

Star Trek fans and writers can overlook the inconsistencies and problems in a first-season episode for two reasons: (1) Because, on the whole, that season is representative of the series' best, and to criticize it would be close to sacreligious; (2) because there is usually enough worthwhile material in a first-season script to compensate for any worthless material.

In "Operation: Annihilate!" for example, neither Spock nor McCoy can remember that one of a sun's properties is light. After Kirk has pointed this out to his scientists, McCoy subjects the Vulcan to a potentially lethal experiment before all preliminary test results have been compiled, needlessly resulting in Spock's blindness. These are professional errors far from "in character" for the best medical mind in Starfleet. The episode would be a total failure were it not for the look at Kirk's family and an excellent example of his strenuous command responsibilities.

In "The Menagerie," Spock shows compassion and practices outright deceit, disobeying Starfleet orders and stealing the *Enterprise* for the sake of his former captain. This flaw in Spock's character, however, is ignored, as "The Menagerie" is otherwise excellent Star Trek—and excellent science fiction.

Like the seasons that preceded it, Star Trek's third contains mistakes—perhaps more than its share. However, it also contains too often overlooked quality drama and science fiction. The episodes commended above are only a few examples of the interesting, sensitive, and important scripts which make it worth looking past the mistakes of the third season to its positive impact on the history of Star Trek.

ALL VULCAN IN ONE TIGHTLY WRAPPED PACKAGE

By Karla Taylor

"So little is known of what went on beneath the surface—so little, yet such a ghastly festering as it bubbles up putrescently in occasional ghoulish glimpses. . . . There was no beauty, no freedom. . . . And inside that rusted iron straitjacket lurked gibbering hideousness, perversion, and diabolism."
—*The Unnamable*, 1925

Howard Phillips Lovecraft was referring to the Puritan of colonial New England, but had he been alive and watching television in September 1967, I feel he would have made this knifelike observation about the world of the Vulcans.

When I first saw "Amok Time," I was a kid. As an adult, I can appreciate Theodore Sturgeon's sly, mordant comment on our own repressed, hedonistic culture.

Much—perhaps too much—has been written about the Vulcans' great shameful secret, the *pon farr*. We were only given a limited amount of information about it, and even that was grudgingly imparted. Apparently it greatly disturbs some fans to think of Vulcans "doing it" only once every seven years. Those people should reread page 227 of *The Making of Star Trek* (original edition), which states: "The specific time interval between these occurrences varies from male to male and by other circumstances. The average is about once every seven Earth years *when a Vulcan is separated from his people as is Spock, more often if living among his own kind.*" (Italics mine) So! It happens more often than every seven years. Does that make anyone happier?

Since Vulcans are fairly humanoid (an ethnocentric term if ever there was one), we can assume that pregnancy takes about the same amount of time as it does for us. Therefore, I very much doubt that *pon farr* would occur more than once a year; two to three years are more likely. What is meant by "other circumstances" is anyone's guess.

We know that *pon farr* is the ignominious underside of Vulcan life, the one thing their logic cannot subdue. We know that it is the "bubbling up" from beneath the cool and stately surface, the price Vulcans pay for their exceedingly repressed lives. This is not mere horniness. It's as much a desire for violence as a desire for sex.

If you take a cooking pot, fill it with water, and place it on the stove with the burner on high, it won't take long to boil. If you then clamp the pot cover down over the pot (kids, don't try this at home) and keep it there, the pot will eventually explode. So it is with such a basic drive as sexuality. Like the old song says, "When an irresistible force meets an immovable object, something's got to give." Indeed. And since love, caring, even good clean lust are verboten among

Vulcans, this exploding desire takes the most violent form—rape. Who can doubt this? The fact that the need is violent as well as sexual is proven by the fact that it can be satisfied by savage, murderous conflict. Besides, if all that was needed was sexual release, masturbation would take care of it.

Of course, technically it's not rape, as Vulcan women are dutiful, willing participants, but that doesn't change the violence.

In another repressed culture, nineteenth-century England, a bride was advised on her wedding night to lie back, close her eyes, and think of Queen Victoria. Maybe Vulcan women are supposed to think of T'Pau. At any rate, pleasure would not be a consideration. What a sick culture! That veneer of civilization is wearing thinner all the time.

This leads to another unanswered question: Since Vulcan women are as repressed as the men, why don't *they* get the *pon farr*? There are two ways to answer this:

Objectively, on American television in the late 1960s, the only sexuality women were allowed was the gooey hearts-and-flowers kind.

Subjectively, I believe that, unlike the men's, Vulcan women's "hormone imbalance" is released bit by bit, during the menstrual cycle. This acts as a safety valve so they never build up to a *pon farr*. (Two hundred years of premenstrual syndrome! One would almost rather have the *pon farr*.) This is the simplest answer, and I believe the best.

Now, about T'Pring, the woman everyone loves to hate. T'Pau was described as "all Vulcan in one package," but I think T'Pring is a better example. This is a woman who has been put into a situation against her will, in which she must arrange other people's deaths in order for a chance of living her own life. Sure, T'Pring is calculating, manipulative, and coldhearted. She must be one of the most popular gals on the planet. But what sort of culture produced this person? Rather a sick one, eh?

By the way, T'Pring's plan may have been flawlessly logical, but she missed two ways her plan could have backfired on her. One, Spock, having won her, might have insisted she accompany him into space (for at least the short time he had left to live) and it would have been "Good-bye Stonn." Two, if Kirk had been the victor, he, being an emotional human, might have taken sweet revenge by marrying her and again taking her back to the ship. She would have had no choice but to go. Being a Vulcan, T'Pring did not take these emotionally based possibilities into account.

Another question: What about Stonn? (Does anyone care?) Why was he apparently free to marry T'Pring? Did his intended bride die? Is he a widower? We'll never know, but my guess is that arranged marriages such as Spock and T'Pring's were only for the upper classes with wealth and prestige to pass along. The average Vulcan may just wait until *pon farr* approaches and then marry—or grab—whoever's available. Again, of course, love or even real desire would not enter into it. Stonn may have been from a lower class and just looking for an "uptown girl."

Poor Spock. He said that he hoped he would be spared the *pon farr*. No doubt. You'd think it would have been the least his human half could have done for him. But, alas, not even that.

Pon farr is, of course, physically intimate, but it's bleakly impersonal. Just how impersonal I will get to shortly. Remember, Spock didn't even have a recent picture of T'Pring. He probably knew virtually nothing about her, and all she knew about him was what she'd read in the papers.

Has anyone but I wondered what went on down there after McCoy, Kirk, and Spock left? All we know is that T'Pau called up the Federation and said, "Please excuse the *Enterprise* for being tardy at your inauguration." That can't be all.

Think about it. The Vulcans were in big trouble. A dead starship captain had just been beamed back to his ship, and his half-Vulcan first officer was about to turn himself in for murder (we always knew he'd be trouble!). The secret of *pon farr* was seriously threatened. This could not be swept under the rug, even with all T'Pau's influence. Now, if Kirk had really been dead, what would they have done?

Would they have sent someone (Sarek?) to dissuade Spock from telling the truth? What else could he have said? Was he planning to commit suicide? We know he wasn't expecting to live much longer. Would the Vulcans even have decided to kill Spock rather than let him testify? (*Tal-shaya?*) That doesn't sound like the (normally) pacifist Vulcans, but everyone has an edge to which they can be pushed.

Frankly, I believe that the secret of *pon farr* will inevitably become known to the Federation at large. As long as Vulcan remains a member and has the inevitable contacts with other races, there will be other beings who'll be putting two and two together. After all, that's what McCoy did. No doubt Christine Chapel did as well. Kirk was a bit slow on the uptake, but that was necessary for the *pon farr* to be explained to the audience. The entire bridge crew saw T'Pring and heard her recitation to Spock. And how many crew members saw the soup incident, and later, the unconscious Kirk before McCoy got him to sickbay? People are people, and one can scarcely imagine a hotter subject for gossip than how Vulcans "do it."

I have a theory about *pon farr*. After giving it some thought, and keeping in mind what an iconoclast Theodore Sturgeon was, I've come to this conclusion about what would have happened if T'Pring had not held up her hand to challenge:

After the brief "wedding ceremony," Spock and T'Pring were going to consummate their marriage right there. In front of everybody.

This would explain several things. First, just before beaming down to Vulcan, Spock told Kirk and McCoy that something, "almost an insanity," occurred at that time, "which you would no doubt find distasteful." It was only after they reassured him that Spock invited them down to the planet with him. Now, by this time both the captain and the doctor understood the basics of *pon farr*. Why, then, this seemingly redundant warning?

Second, it would explain T'Pau's strange attitude toward Kirk and McCoy. The first thing she asked Spock was, "Are our ceremonies for outworlders?" A tight attitude, even for a Vulcan, to what was going to be just a brief ceremony, eh?

T'Pau's attitude toward Spock was one of scarcely disguised contempt, but her attitude toward the two outworlders was different: challenging. As if she were saying, "This is how we do things here and I dare you to be shocked at anything you see." ("What thee are about to see . . .") Why so portentous? At that point T'Pau believed all would go as usual, for T'Pring had not yet challenged. "This is our way," concluded T'Pau to Kirk and McCoy, and her tone was very challenging indeed. What did she think they were about to witness?

Third, we know that the story's author, Theodore Sturgeon, went into great detail with this scene, deciding even what sort of clothes the Vulcans would wear. Remember T'Pring's dress? How oddly it was cut up the front? Was that just style or accommodation?

Fourth, and this relates to the previous point, the setting was very much based on a circular megalithic henge, like Stonehenge or Avebury in England. Historians know that many of the ceremonies held in these places involved public sex (fertility rites, ritual marriages, etc.). I believe Theodore Sturgeon was well aware of this.

Fifth, about the time T'Pring challenged, Spock went into the *plak tow* state. He would have done this, of course, even if she hadn't challenged ("almost an insanity"). Now, given that desperately feverish madness, it seems extremely unlikely that following the marriage ceremony, Spock would have been able to just leave the temple area and walk away with the wedding party to a house or other enclosed, private place. No, this was it. There and then. Let the games begin, as they said in ancient Rome.

Sixth, consummation in front of everyone would certainly help keep sex impersonal and purely physical. Private sex might foster real passion, which is obviously something Vulcans wish to avoid.

This is far into speculation, but would help explain just how deeply humiliating *pon farr* is for Vulcans, and why Spock warned off his friends even as he invited them along.

I have yet another way of looking at "Amok Time." It is an allegory of rabies.

Rabies (from the Latin *rabere*, "to rage"), is also called hydrophobia (Greek, "fear of water") and the deceptively lovely word *lyssa* (Greek, "frenzy"). It's doubtful that *pon farr* has any ulterior meaning, but "ponos" is Greek for "pain." Rabies attacks the central nervous system, including, of course, the brain. The disease is one basis for the legends of werewolves. The disease progresses in three stages:

1. Premonitory stage—depression, anxiety, increased nervousness. Lasts about two days.

2. Excitement stage—increased irritability, hypersensitivity, confusion, paranoia. Increasing feelings of panic and terror, intensified by difficult breathing and swallowing. The victim refuses food and drink and can react violently to offers and even mention of water, thus the name "hydrophobia." Excitement increases to a demented rage, and attacks on others are not uncommon. Victims often show a marked desire to be left alone. Retching, pallor, and high fever ensue. Lasts one to four days.

3. Terminal stage—paralysis and unconsciousness ensue and the victim dies. Lasts only a matter of hours.

The opening scene of the program shows Spock

literally throwing Nurse Chapel out of his cabin when she goes in to offer him some soup. (Soup is, of course, mostly water.)

Spock obviously became more nervous and hypertensive as time went on, and showed signs of potential violence (threatening to break the doctor's neck); confusion (not remembering that he ordered a course change); and even paranoia (against Chapel—"If I want something from you, I'll ask for it!") and against McCoy (extreme reluctance to be examined). He wasn't eating. His entire mind was turned to the thought of hiding away by himself until he could get to Vulcan. Even after he thought he'd never get there, Spock still wished to be locked away.

Of course, eventually we saw a demented rage exhibited, coinciding with high fever.

Fortunately, Spock never reached the third stage, but he would have, had Kirk just confined him and gone on to the inauguration.

Once you start peeling away that veneer of civilization, Vulcan society no longer appears as that cool, elegant image it wants to project. Not a nice place to visit, and I wouldn't like to live there.

Where does this leave Sarek and Amanda? They are certainly among the most fortunate people in the Star Trek universe. They are happier than Jim Kirk, on a one-way road to old age littered with the wrecks of past affairs. They are happier than T'Pring, chained for life to a dullard. And, a sad irony, they are infinitely happier than their own son.

Perhaps those "other circumstances" apply to them.

ASK NOT WHAT YOUR FEDERATION CAN DO FOR YOU: KIRK AS A KENNEDY FIGURE

by Judy Klass

Star Trek has demonstrated a staying power that few television shows can equal and none can top. By stubbornly remaining in syndication, spawning new major motion pictures, and continually attracting a new, younger following, it proves its timeless ability to move people and to make them think. Star Trek refuses to become dated. Yet Star Trek is also an unusually rich source for insights into the era in which it was created. Since nearly twenty years have passed since the first episodes were aired, it is possible to use this show of the future to look back at the dreams and ideas of the 1960s. In the context of that period in history, Star Trek was in many ways ahead of its time, but also in many ways a catharsis for traumas of that decade.

Gene Roddenberry, as we know, had ambitious hopes for his brainchild to advocate change, to reflect social and political movements of the times. To a degree he was successful. In terms of sexual politics, the network killed his suggested female officer, but the show did manage to present strong women such as Number One (in the footage from "The Cage" used in "The Menagerie") and the Romulan commander in "The *Enterprise*

Incident." Lieutenant Uhura's ability to strike a proud blow for women and for blacks was as limited as her role often was. But Dr. Daystrom in "The Ultimate Computer" was a strongly drawn character, a genius who had designed the components of the *Enterprise*. In a decade when Sidney Poitier raged against never being offered a role that a white actor could have played as easily—in which race was not an issue—color was quite irrelevant in "The Ultimate Computer." And with science fiction as a metaphor, Star Trek was able to forcefully tackle issues such as Vietnam and the cold war, drugs, and the generation gap, which were usually considered too hot for TV.

Since sundry writers wrote Star Trek episodes, different points of view are seen. The episode "A Private Little War" cannot be viewed as anything but a rationalization for our involvement in Vietnam. "Errand of Mercy," on the other hand, gently mocks the arrogance of superpowers that lets their quarrels with each other spill into their relations with supposedly inferior cultures. We all recognize, after all, on some level, that the Klingons and, to a degree, the Romulans, are thinly veiled Russians, cosmic communist aggressors. Even as Star Trek offered a vision of hope, of mankind having survived the nuclear age and turned pioneer once again, the uneasy traditions of the twentieth century crept into the vision.

"Charlie X," "Miri," and even the ill-conceived "And the Children Shall Lead" all reflect problems caused by the generation gap. The ludicrous episode "The Way to Eden," with its space hippies running amok, can only be viewed now as an extremely camp, far-out period piece. (The best way to watch it is to make a bowl of popcorn, sit around with friends, and laugh at the wonderful silliness of it.) "This Side of Paradise," "The Naked Time," who knows, even "Shore Leave" perhaps, touch on the attention that hallucinogenic drugs were receiving at that time.

A few small touches here and there, such as Mr. Chekov's incongruous Beatle haircut the second season, the micro-skirts of the crew women, and the flower-children outfits of many of the primitive peoples that the *Enterprise* encountered, remind us of the years in which the shows were made. As for the general look of the show—considering the minimal budget they had for special effects—it holds up very well. In the wake of *Star Wars*, most Fifties and Sixties science fiction films and TV shows tend to look like so much crockery stuck together with Scotch tape.

One thing we must remember about Star Trek is that it was made in the late 1960s, a very disturbing time, when many of our basic assumptions about our society were being questioned, when people felt disillusioned, lost. Many people date the beginning of national chaos, the dashing of dreams, with the 1963 assassination of President John F. Kennedy in Dallas. It is my contention that Captain James T. Kirk of the Starship *Enterprise* took up Kennedy's fallen torch in the subconscious minds of countless viewers.

Obviously, Kirk wasn't designed to be a Kennedy figure. After all, the captain of the *Enterprise* was originally to be Captain Christopher Pike, played by Jeffrey Hunter. All I'm saying is, after Kirk's character had been created and William Shatner cast in the role, something clicked. There is even a superficial physical resemblance between Shatner and Kennedy.

Certainly the optimism and adventurous spirit of the show seemed to harken back to the JFK years. As Kennedy had sought to chart a New Frontier, so Kirk would explore "Space, the final frontier." A frontier that would never end.

Kennedy's life was cut short, and, like Kennedy, Kirk was killed on several occasions, but Kirk always got better. In "The Tholian Web," "The Enterprise Incident," "Amok Time," his smile is always back to reassure us by the final frame. Attempts to assassinate him on the *Enterprise* in "Journey to Babel" and "Mirror, Mirror" are duly thwarted.

It's well known that JFK was intrigued by space exploration and was a strong proponent of NASA. And he was a powerful public speaker, as Kirk is often shown to be.

President Kennedy was a curious political combination. He projected the image of a liberal reformer, but also of a hard-line cold warrior. Kirk projects the same duality. America takes a paternalistic, rather patronizing view toward Third World countries sometimes. We ignore their national heritages, some might argue, and expect them to model themselves eagerly on our society. Kennedy pursued such ends through organizations such as the Organization of American States (OAS) and the Alliance for Progress. We become frustrated when smaller countries choose a different path than the one we point out to them. It is refreshing for us, in Star Trek, to see Kirk so easily breeze onto different planets and reconstitute their governments so that they will evolve into suitable members of the United Federation of Planets.

There are two contradictory myths about President

Kennedy that somehow manage to happily coexist. One is of the sincere young politician, the family man devoted to Jackie and the kids. The other is of JFK the international stud (with conquests such as Marilyn Monroe), the James Bond-type charmer who was not afraid of taking some unorthodox political risks if he felt that the end justified the means.

Likewise, Kirk is an honorable officer obsessed by his ship. He is the finest that the Federation has. Yet he is also generally acknowledged as a "cosmic womanizer" who does not hesitate to play fast and loose with the Prime Directive.

The boyish charm, the youth of a man like Kennedy (or Kirk), is a great asset. In "The Deadly Years," the practical threat is that the radiation-ravaged Kirk cannot function. But in this episode, which Shatner so disliked making, the real threat is the image of a vigorous, handsome young leader usurped by a belligerent, incompetent old one, as Kennedy had given way to Johnson, even as the generation gap widened. Fortunately, by the end of the episode, youth and style are back in the saddle once more.

What, then, of the rest of the *Enterprise* crew? If Kirk is JFK, who is Spock, you ask? Bobby? Well, it's possible. Kirk and Spock speak of each other to "Lord" Garth as being brothers. Throughout his brother's life, Bobby Kennedy was content to remain in his shadow; it seemed he had "no wish to command." So what would that make McCoy? Obviously, I know it is easy to stretch this theory way out of proportion. The Kirk/ Spock relationship, in all its wonderful complexity, should not be forced into so one-dimensional a mold.

Star Trek has much more substance than do the specters of one mythical Administration.

However, if we want to stretch things a bit more, surely "The Corbomite Maneuver" can be seen as a way of vicariously replaying the Cuban Missile Crisis. And why not? To many, it was Kennedy's finest hour, and Kirk masterfully uses style, bluff, and timing just as JFK did. And Kirk inspires admiration in Charlie X and Miri, just as Kennedy did in young people of his day.

If people in the late 1960s felt their lives had lost focus, Star Trek offered them a porthole to an alternative way of life. A life of the future, where people did not live in the shadow of the Bomb, where the establishment was flexible and acceptable and just, where high ideals could be realized, and where there would be a spiritual rebirth. It's a vision that grew directly out of the cynicism and despair of the era.

In creating the universe of tomorrow, Star Trek may have been partially trying to recapture a moment of the past, unconsciously trying to recapture the aspirations of a fallen president, and to rescue the vision of Camelot untarnished from a world gone mad and carry it majestically up into the stars.

UNIFORMS

by Lieutenant David Crockett

Through television and motion pictures Star Trek has presented to us nearly thirty years of Starfleet and Federation history. In a time period that long, change is inevitable. The Starfleet we see today only remotely resembles the fleet of Captain Christopher Pike. There are different ways in which one could examine the many changes, but one of the easier and more definitive ways is to examine the uniforms of Star Trek.

Uniforms have always been a staple of organized military life, and Starfleet is no exception. Although the primary mission of the *Enterprise* and like vessels is that of scientific exploration and alien contact, starships cover a host of secondary missions—military, diplomatic, etc.—and their organization illustrates this fact. Starship crew members progress through an established rank structure in specific branches. Uniforms reflect that progression, for they tell us both the rank of an individual and his branch of service, roughly equivalent to one's area of expertise.

The uniforms of Star Trek have changed much over the years. By examining this evolution from the days of Captain Pike to those of Captain Spock, we can learn much about the careers of the *Enterprise* crew, the organization of Starfleet, and the fleet's changing role over the years.

Let us start at the beginning, and the beginning of Star Trek rests with what seems to us now to be an almost ancient *Enterprise* under the command of a young Captain Christopher Pike. There are only two prominent uniform colors during this time—blue and golden yellow—but there are at least three specific branches, or divisions. The insignia of the *Enterprise* herself is the familiar arrowhead shape. The branch symbols are found in the middle of this insignia. Command is represented by a star, sciences by a three-dimensional ring, and support services by a jagged spiral. At this time, those branched sciences wear blue shirts, while those in command and support both wear the yellow. Captain Pike and First Officer Number One are both branched command. As science officer, Spock is naturally branched sciences. The same is true for Phillip Boyce, the ship's Chief Medical Officer. Lieutenant Tyler, who mans the helm, is in support.

Rank designation at this time is very general. This is evident when one notices that Captain Pike, Number One, Doctor Boyce, and Lieutenants Spock and Tyler all wear one solid gold stripe to indicate rank. Captain Pike is the acknowledged senior officer, but his rank does not reflect this. The single gold stripe probably indicates the very general designation of officer. This differentiates them from the plain cuffs of the crewmen.

The uniforms of this early voyage tell us some interesting things about Starfleet. From the episode "The Menagerie," we know this to be thirteen years prior to

Spock's trial; it is a full twenty-eight years before the *Enterprise* herself is destroyed. (Admiral Morrow's comment in *The Search for Spock* about the *Enterprise* being twenty years old is a gross underestimate. She's at least thirty.) The Federation at this time seems to have just commenced a new era of widened exploration and expansion, and the *Enterprise* is its finest ship. She is undoubtedly a fairly new vessel, possibly having just completed her shake-down cruise under her new commander, Robert April. The division of branches indicates that Starfleet is well established and organized, but the simplified rank designation makes it apparent that it is a young organizational structure. Captain Pike represents the beginning of that era in Starfleet when the starship and her crew enjoyed the utmost flexibility and independence from Headquarters —a true Horatio Hornblower in space, brought to its highest level by James T. Kirk.

About twelve years later, the *Enterprise* finds herself under the command of Captain Kirk. Neither the ship nor the uniforms have changed much since the early days of Captain Pike, but some things should be noted, as they set the stage for the first five-year mission under Kirk.

In "Where No Man Has Gone Before," Spock is seen wearing the command branch insignia on a yellow shirt. This is the first indication of an essential fact: As members of any military organization advance in rank and responsibility, they must attend advanced schooling to remain qualified. Sometime in the recent past, perhaps even while Pike was in command, Spock was made first officer of the *Enterprise*. This greatly increased his duties, since he remained science officer as well. In order to fully qualify for both jobs, Spock probably attended an advanced command course. He then transferred from sciences to command for a time. This placed him irrevocably on the road to an eventual command of his own. Now that he is command-qualified, he will soon transfer back to sciences, his true vocation.

This episode also marks the entrance of Sulu and Scotty. Sulu is head of the astrosciences department and is branched sciences, while Chief Engineer Scott is branched support. As chief medical officer, Doctor Mark Piper is also head of the Life Sciences department and branched sciences. That position will soon be filled by Doctor McCoy. Finally, Chief Navigator Gary Mitchell is branched support.

One annoying thing about this episode, which must be taken into account for those who pay great attention to detail, is that the sciences and life-support insignia are reversed from the rest of the series. That is, scientists Sulu, Piper, and Dehner wear the jagged spiral of support, while support personnel Scott, Mitchell, and Kelso wear the three-dimensional ring of sciences. Though it is perhaps best to ignore this inconsistency, there is a feeble explanation that can be given for those who insist on rationalizing such things. For an unknown reason, probably the birth of modern Starfleet bureaucracy, sciences and support switched their insignia sometime during Pike's command, only to switch them back during Kirk's command. . . . Perhaps we should just forget it.

Rank insignia at this time is only slightly more specific than before. Sometime during the few preceding years, Starfleet decided to set apart the commander of the ship. As captain, therefore, Kirk now wears two solid stripes on his sleeve as opposed to the single stripe worn by his officers. As first officer, Spock has been promoted to lieutenant commander, but his uniform still bears a single stripe.

The first major change in modern Starfleet history takes place immediately following "Where No Man Has Gone Before." The *Enterprise* herself undergoes a thorough refitting. There are internal changes, and the crew complement is more than doubled from the 203 of Pike's command to the 430 of Kirk's. The biggest change is in the uniforms.

The three major branches remain, their insignia intact. Now, however, uniform color is directly related to branch. Yellow shirts correspond to command, blue shirts to sciences, and the new red shirts to support. Spock therefore has completed his transfer from command back to sciences; Sulu has completed a transfer from sciences to command as he takes his position at the helm. Uhura very early on is seen branched command, but she soon transfers to support. Doctor McCoy takes his place as chief medical officer, and is joined by Nurse Chapel, who brings evidence of yet a fourth branch in Starfleet, the medical branch. This is indicated by the red cross on her *Enterprise* insignia. It would seem, then, that the chief medical officer, because he is also head of Life Sciences, is normally branched sciences, whereas strictly medical personnel have a separate branch to themselves. Their slightly different uniform style supports this statement. Finally, it should be noted that Yeoman Rand begins her career in support.

Rank insignia has also become more specific. Lieutenants Sulu and Uhura wear one solid stripe, while Lieutenant Commanders Scott and McCoy wear one solid and one broken stripe. Chekov, when he first appears as an ensign branched command, wears no rank insignia. As captain, Kirk wears two solid stripes surrounding one broken stripe. Spock, meanwhile, poses a problem. He wears two solid stripes, indicating his eventual rank of commander, but early on he is clearly referred to as a lieutenant commander. This same situation exists for Records Officer Finney and Security Chief Giotto. All three men are identified in episodes as lieutenant commanders, yet all three wear commander's stripes. It is certain that the rank of commander is a step above lieutenant commander and not simply a title honoring position. Probably these three men hold brevet ranks, awaiting Starfleet action to become official. Spock is soon a commander in rank as well as position.

The most startling uniform change at this time is that of the female uniform, for better or worse, depending on your point of view. This inexplicable change from trousers to short skirts is never adequately explained or justified. Perhaps it marks either the beginning of Starfleet's decline or the culmination of its ascent. The debate continues.

Let us now see what the preceding changes tell us about Starfleet at the time of the first five-year mission under Captain Kirk. Just as there is an upgrading of technology, so there is a change in organization. This is most noticeable at the helm. Before this time the helm positions were manned by officers in support. Now, however, the helm is a command position. Sulu's change from physicist to helmsman indicates an ambition to eventually command a starship. Because the reorganized Starfleet specified that the helm would now be a command position, Sulu takes this opportunity.

It is now clear that branch determines job, but note should be made that there are exceptions to this in the operational procedures of the *Enterprise*. All officers on the ship are cross-trained so they can perform several jobs if necessary. Thus, both Uhura and Kyle are seen manning the helm at times. Chekov is being trained in sciences, for he is often seen at Spock's station. There are many times when a primary officer of the bridge crew is missing, even during a red-alert emergency. When such cases occur, the officer in question is elsewhere on the ship, performing alternate duties or manning backup systems. There also occur occasional instances in which branch assignment seems incongruous with job. For instance, Doctor Anne Mulhall, an astrobiologist, is branched support. Under normal circumstances she would be in sciences, but apparently her job aboard the *Enterprise* is support-oriented.

We now know something about the normal career progression of Starfleet officers. It is easy to see that they are cross-trained in the fundamentals of several jobs. This is an obvious necessity for the bridge crew, whom we see most often, and an indication of their special level of skill and expertise. It seems that young officers are marked for a specific assignment upon commissioning, but there is also a certain flexibility concerning job and branch that enables one to pursue the development most suited to that person. Spock, Sulu, and Uhura all change their positions in Starfleet one way or another, and it will soon be shown that other changes also occur.

Starfleet now appears more centralized and bureaucratized than before, and it is beginning to threaten the independence of the Hornblower-minded Kirk. Several times he runs up against the wall of Starfleet organization. Nevertheless, the ensuing five-year mission of the *Enterprise* is one of unprecedented discovery and expansion for the Federation. It is also one of unprecedented disaster for Starfleet. The primary mission of the *Enterprise* remains to explore and contact alien life. Consider the contacts made in less than five years: Talosians, Thasians, Metrons, Vians, Excalbians, Lactrans, Organians, Melkotians. Include also Trelane, Apollo, Sargon, Kukulkan. Include also the giant space amoeba and the doomsday machine. Alien life of such power is bound to give any military mind concerned with Federation security a massive headache, despite the fact that many of the above proved either benevolent or remarkably disinterested in the rest of the galaxy. A few pose enough of a threat to be potentially devastating should they ever turn truly belligerent.

As the *Enterprise* pushed back the boundaries of the Federation, she also pushed back the feeling of security provided by the expanse of space. In addition to the alien life mentioned above, consider also that of the twelve or thirteen *Enterprise*-type ships in the fleet, three were completely destroyed—*Constellation, Intrepid, Defiant*—and two rendered devoid of life—*Exeter* and *Excalibur*—in little more than a year. To put this in perspective, imagine the United States losing five of its nuclear aircraft carriers or five of its army divisions. It is a major disaster for Starfleet, for it is a loss of over a third of the starship fleet. It is extremely difficult to absorb the loss of over two thousand starship personnel. In the face of these events, we can only increase our admiration of Captain Kirk and his crew for bringing in the *Enterprise* relatively unscathed. We have grown accustomed to thinking of the *Enterprise* as representative of Starfleet; that view perhaps gives too much credit to the fleet and not enough to the character of the *Enterprise* crew and the people who lead them.

Nevertheless, it is obvious why at the conclusion of this famous five-year mission, Starfleet again undergoes a tremendous change. The results are seen almost three years later, as Vejur heads menacingly toward Earth. The *Enterprise* has been refitted again, this time dramatically so. Starfleet uniforms are also greatly changed. There are several styles: long-sleeved or short-sleeved, one-piece or two-piece, brown or blue, or otherwise. Uniform color is no longer pertinent to branch, and they are unisexual once again. Rank insignia remains the same, and most of the old *Enterprise* crew have been promoted one rank.

The major changes occur in branch selection. By this time the old branch insignia have been replaced. The star of command has become the universal insignia of the *Enterprise*. Branch is now indicated by the background color of the new *Enterprise* insignia. A white background indicates command, red indicates engineering, yellow indicates support, and green indicates medical. Special notice should be taken that engineering has been reorganized into a separate branch.

Admiral Kirk and Captain Decker both wear the white of command. Lieutenant Chekov, absent from the *Enterprise* during the latter part of its mission to train for his present assignment as security and weapons officer (demonstrated by his absence from the animated series), is also branched command. Doctor McCoy, following his "forced induction" back into the *Enterprise* crew, has transferred to the medical branch. This may be due to his extensive research into the applications of Fabrini medicine. Lieutenant Commander Sulu, however, has been transferred from command to support. When Spock rejoins the *Enterprise*, he is branched engineering, as are Chief Engineer Scott and Transporter Chief Rand.

The positions of Ilia, Sulu, Chekov, and Spock are evidence of more organizational change in Starfleet. The helm positions held by Ilia and Sulu were support positions in the early days of the *Enterprise*, but during Kirk's first command they were changed to command positions. Now they have returned to their former branch. This is Sulu's third known branch. While diverse training is good, it must also be complementary. Constant branch changing, particularly while holding the same job, can lead to bureaucratic nightmares, and is not conducive to rapid advancement. Starfleet reorganization quite possibly costs Sulu an early starship command, a position he certainly merits but does not receive until it is too late. Chekov's position, on the other hand, indicates that the security forces of Starfleet have been moved from the support branch to command. Chekov's wide experience and continuity in the command branch structure certainly contributes to his promotion to first officer of the *Reliant* years later.

As for the engineering branch of Spock, the explanation lies in the nature of the refitted starship. Due to the highly advanced nature of the engineering, the new transporter, and new pulse-warp drive, the refitting involved many scientific problems and theories. The engineering section, at least that of the *Enterprise*, became a branch separate from support. When Spock rejoins the *Enterprise*, the engines are the major source of concern. Though he is listed as the ship's science officer, for the rest of this voyage and the remainder of the refitting he is technically branched engineering. This situation is similar to that mentioned earlier concerning Dr. Anne Mulhall's peculiar position.

This is a good time to mention yet another indication of Starfleet's reorganization. When Kirk is promoted, he is not promoted to the rank of commodore, which is the next highest rank after captain, but to the rank of admiral. The commodores of Starfleet, represented by such people as Commodores Stone, Mendez, Barstow, Decker, Stocker, Wesley, and April bore three solid stripes to designate rank. They commanded starbases, fleet task forces, and held high-level staff positions. What seems to have happened in the reshuffle at Starfleet is that the rank of commodore has been eliminated, to be replaced by another grade of admiral, of which there are several. This is not that unusual, for the United States Navy did the same thing following World War II. As a result, there never was a Commodore James T. Kirk.

At the end of *Star Trek: The Motion Picture*, the Star Trek universe again seems to be in order. Kirk is again in command of the Federation's finest crew on Starfleet's finest vessel, prepared for another five-year mission. The mission of the *Enterprise* continues to be one primarily of science. By the time Khan Noonian Singh and Commander Kruge arrive to wreak havoc on all, however, this has completely changed. We know that the death of Spock and subsequent destruction of the *Enterprise* takes place nearly eight years after the Vejur incident. This is very apparent when one considers the dramatic change in uniform style and the fact that the *Enterprise*, at the cutting edge of Federation technology a few years prior, is now only fit (ostensibly) for the scrap heap.

The uniforms have now undergone their third major change. They are much more military in style than any of the previous ones. The *Enterprise* insignia is universally present on all belts. This includes members of other starships and starbase personnel. There was a time, during the series, when fleet personnel not assigned to a starship bore a different insignia. In fact, even other starships sported unique designs. Now, however, the *Enterprise* symbol is omnipresent. The old rank stripes have been replaced by metallic insignia worn on the right shoulder. Finally, branch is now identified by the color of the right shoulder strap and the color of the underlying sweater. Command, support, sciences, and medical still retain their colors—white, yellow, blue, and green, respectively—while engineering has returned again to support.

Admiral Kirk remains in command, but he is now

joined by Captain Spock, who is the new commander of the *Enterprise*. Other commanders—Terrell, Styles, Esteban, Morrow—also wear white. It is interesting to note that in the brief glimpse we have of Janice Rand, she is ranked a commander and is branched command. Considering her origin as a yeoman just fifteen years ago, this is a remarkable achievement. In the meantime, McCoy remains branched medical. Commander Sulu remains in support, but, if we are to believe the movie novelization and the assumption of a promotion to captain for him, he will soon change to the white of command. This is also assuming his career survives the hijacking of a starship. Scott as well rejoins the support branch, and maintains it even as captain of engineering of *Excelsior*. Commander Chekov, in his new position as science officer of the *Reliant*, has been transferred to sciences. This is hardly surprising, considering his close work with Spock when he first joined the *Enterprise* bridge crew. It has long been known that he is well trained in this area. Joining Chekov on the *Reliant* is Commander Kyle, one-time transporter chief of the *Enterprise*, also now branched sciences. Commander Uhura, after fifteen years in support and several more years before that in command, is now branched sciences.

The one remaining person, Lieutenant Saavik, poses a problem. In *The Wrath of Khan*, she and her fellow trainees wear both red and black collars. This could simply designate status, black representing perhaps Academy cadets (midshipmen) or ensigns, and red representing young lieutenants training for their first starship assignment. Saavik, being a lieutenant, wears red. In *The Search for Spock*, however, she wears the white of command. Her duties on the *Grissom* indicate that she should be wearing the blue of sciences. It is possible that her assignment to the *Grissom* is intended to be only temporary, for the duration of the Genesis expedition. Her situation would not be unlike that of Anne Mulhall's or Spock's during the Vejur incident.

It is obvious that Starfleet has undergone yet another reorganization, this one more drastic than the last. The communications specialty, represented with great skill by Uhura, has been completely transferred to the sciences branch. This is perhaps due to the nature of modern communications, particularly with the development of the so-called transwarp drive. The position of Scotty as captain of engineering on board the *Excelsior* indicates something else about the new direction Starfleet is taking. With the advent of larger and apparently more powerful starships, department heads like engineering, life sciences and astrosciences will now hold the rank of captain, while remaining in that specific branch, and be under the overall command of a senior captain, such as Captain Styles.

This new Starfleet bears little resemblance to the organization that pioneered galactic exploration thirty years ago. Indeed, the period of wide and rapid exploration seems to have ended. Starfleet has now taken on the role of military protector. Interstellar politics have stripped starship commanders of their independence. One only has to examine the actions of Captain Styles and Captain Esteban, as well as Admiral Morrow, to realize that this is so. Captain Kirk, had he been on the *Grissom*, would never have "checked with Starfleet" before beaming up a Vulcan child in a snowstorm. The lack of initiative and general malaise, reaching to the highest level, is glaring. The presence of vessels like *Reliant* and *Grissom* suggest that the scientific mission of the *Enterprise* has been transferred to others. The *Enterprise* herself has been relegated to the role of training vessel. The existence of the *Excelsior* brings with it the possibility of a new era of intergalactic exploration, but its full potential still remains to be seen.

What, then, does the future hold for the former crew of the starship *Enterprise*? Assume they are not all brought to trial for mutiny, aiding in the escape of a Federation prisoner, the disabling of one starship, hijacking and then destroying another, and breaking the quarantine on the planet Genesis. Assume they do not flee to deep space to become benevolent pirates. Assume instead that somehow all is set right and they even get a new ship, perhaps even a new *Enterprise*. What then? Professional advancement cannot be ignored.

At the present time, the following situation exists among the legendary crew: Admiral Kirk, acting always like a captain and never an admiral, certainly wants a command. Mister Spock, however, has already been promoted to captain. To continue, Scott has also attained the rank of captain, as has Sulu. Chekov is a first officer, just one step away from being a captain. Uhura is a commander, just one rank below a captain, though it is uncertain what her next career move might be. At any rate, of the seven major characters, four are already captains or higher, with two more close behind. We can safely assume that Doctor McCoy will stay away from command—unless he becomes "Captain of Life Sciences." An interesting, even fascinating idea.

Shall we have a crew run by a group of captains? As the fourth movie approaches, the future of our favorite crew remains much in doubt. Considering the path the stories have taken, Starfleet and its uniforms will probably not change significantly in *Star Trek IV*. The characters, however, have reached the point at which some tough decisions must be made. It will be interesting to see what direction they will take.

THE EMPATH

by Tom Lalli

"The Empath" is one of the best-realized episodes of
Star Trek and one that has long intrigued me, not least
because of the lack of attention it receives in nonfic-
tion articles. Though it elicits strong feelings, both
positive and negative, in many fans, it is also rarely
seen on lists of the best or worst shows. (Often it is
remembered for McCoy's "I'm a doctor, not a coal
miner.")

Perhaps this is because we just don't know what to
make of "The Empath." It is a unique show: subdued,
surreal, and theatrical. There is no deadline to be met,
no threat to the galaxy or to the *Enterprise* (actually,
there *is* a deadline, but it is the Vians' deadline, not
ours). Instead we have a mystery-drama played out
among six beings; this is very unusual for Star Trek.
The darkened stage on which the play is presented
makes the experience even stranger, and it's clear that
"The Empath" is rich in symbolism.

Accordingly, the episode is enigmatic in the extreme. This alone, I think, makes it attractive, because
it is so rare for something on television to be *difficult
to understand*. Of course, Star Trek fans are used to

subtle and thought-provoking fare, but still, even for Star Trek, "The Empath" is quite obscure. The fact that the show was produced in the third season may also seem odd. However, that year did see some original and intelligent shows produced. For those seeking a reason for the success of "The Empath" amid the mediocrity of the last year, perhaps the fact that the show was co-produced by Robert Justman (who had been with the show since the first season) will suffice.

As "The Empath" opens, the *Enterprise* is traveling to Minara 2 to pick up the staff of a research station placed there to observe the system's sun (which is about to nova). Kirk, Spock, and McCoy arrive at the small research building and find it deserted, the instruments covered in dust. A record tape left behind shows the two scientists becoming bored with their assignment; Dr. Linke call the plant a "God-forsaken place." This is immediately followed by a ground tremor. His colleague, Dr. Ozaba, apparently a religious or literary man, quotes the Bible: " 'In his hand are the deep places of the earth [: the strength of the hills is his also].' " Psalm ninety-five, verse four—looks like he [God] was listening." Actually, the tremor's cause is the imminent nova (there will be another tremor later), but this religious reference signals the presence of some powerful, lurking force, i.e., the Vians.

On the tape viewer, the two scientists disappear from the station; soon, Kirk, Spock, and McCoy also disappear in like fashion. Obviously, whatever happened to the scientists is happening to them. This is the teaser. After the commercial pause, we see the titles "The Empath" and "By Joyce Muskat," in white on a black screen. Again, this is very unusual for Star

Trek. Throughout the episode, the surrounding blackness makes whatever we are watching stand out. Next, there is a sharp cut to Kirk, Spock, and McCoy lying on the floor.

The *Enterprise* crewmen now pick up where the research crew left off: they are rational, scientific, and inquisitive. The very purpose of the Federation's presence on the planet is scientific research; now the three men attack their problem with scientific logic. This is shown in their technical dialogue, the professionalism of their behavior, and the use of the tricorder.

The three *Enterprise* crewmen try to determine what is going on by using deductive logic. Gem, in contrast, is intuitive and unintellectual. Kirk and his men, as we shall see, lie between the soulless Vians and the soulful Gem. They soon discover that rationality will not be enough to get them out of this predicament. The three must use their emotions, especially their emotional bonds with one another, to satisfy the Vians and thus escape. Some other Federation officers would not have been able to escape, no matter how proficient they were at their tasks, without the emotional bonds these three enjoy. But then, perhaps the Vians chose Kirk, Spock, and McCoy with this fact in mind.

Linke and Ozaba, we soon discover, are dead, apparently from torture. We fear that the same is intended for our heroes. The Vians qualify this conclusion; of the researchers they say, "Their own fears and weaknesses killed them." In retrospect, we can see that this probably means they died because they were not willing to sacrifice themselves for each other, and thus were unable to teach Gem to help them. They lacked reasons to help each other, and thus could not impart any such reason to Gem. All this becomes obvious when we see Gem look at the two dead men; she is emotionless, without compassion or even recognition. As the episode progresses, we see Gem become increasingly concerned with the feelings of others.

At this point, though, Kirk (and we) don't know what the Vians' purpose (if any) is. Kirk assumes that *Gem* knows the purpose: ". . . and she knows." Kirk habitually makes such assumptions, as with Odona in "Mark of Gideon." Our clues to the mystery, however, come not from Gem but from the cryptic statements of the Vians. "They love life greatly to struggle so." "Yes, the prime ingredient." "Your will to survive, your love of life, your will to know . . . each of you will give your lives for the other—now we must see if Gem will do the same." This last line, coming during the weird, slow-motion scene on the planet's surface, is the first real explanation we (and Kirk) receive.

The mysteriousness of the Vians makes even more disturbing the dangerous position in which the three men find themselves. Perhaps more than any other episode, "The Empath" makes us fear for the lives of the Big Three. The humiliation and helplessness of Kirk is particularly disorienting. Kirk, Star Trek's pillar of strength, is the character we see victimized and abused, helpless. Also in this show we finally see a mirage (Scotty and the rescue party) disturbing Spock's "mathematically perfect brain waves"—he too is vulnerable.

One of the most significant moments in "The Empath" occurs when Gem touches Spock's shoulder and reads his thoughts and feelings. At first she is disturbed by what she senses in him. She feels Spock worrying about his captain, and probably his fears for himself as well (perhaps it is also his alienness which upsets her). She then smiles at him with sympathy and understanding, thus confirming the fact that Spock is very attractive to females. The Vulcan raises his eyebrow at this display of affection. The original script had Gem being repelled by what she felt inside Spock; for obvious reasons, this was changed. Gem is learning what compassion and friendship mean.

Gem helps Kirk to recover, but she pulls back at one point. "Her withdrawal would suggest fear of death," Spock suggests. McCoy responds, "Maybe she doesn't know our captain well enough yet to offer up her life for him." This sardonic comment will soon take on added significance when McCoy's life depends upon Gem. We see Kirk in an unusually submissive posture. All he can do is say thank you to Gem. (The similarity between "Gem" and "Jim" belies the fact that she learns from each of the three men.)

Spock then suggests using the Vian device. McCoy, still caught up in the emotion of the situation (as we are), blurts out, "Spock, why do you have to get so analytical at a time like this?" McCoy says it kindly, though, out of habit rather than harshness. These three men really care about one another, which is why they can comfort each other with such bantering. Linke and Ozaba probably worked together well, but they did not love each other as Kirk, Spock, and McCoy do.

Now the Vians need a subject, either Spock or McCoy. McCoy will probably die (85% chance), while Spock will live but probably suffer permanent brain damage resulting in insanity (93% chance). Here we have the kind of moral quandary which was often presented in Star Trek. As in "Operation: Annihilate," Kirk puts off the decision, insisting that there be an alternative. McCoy, taking matters into his own hands, puts Kirk to sleep.

Spock immediately understands why McCoy has given Kirk the shot. But poor Spock is still naive when it comes to human trickery; McCoy soon hypos him also. "Your action is highly unethical" is Spock's response this time. The beauty of this scene is that the two characters are fighting over the privilege of being tortured. And it *is* a privilege, because each would rather suffer the consequences than live knowing that his friend went in his place. McCoy wins the battle— "Not this time, Mister Spock"—and goes off with the Vians. The fact that McCoy is the least outwardly heroic of the three makes even more appropriate his role as Gem's teacher.

When McCoy leaves, Gem realizes what he is doing and she cries. These may be her first tears. She now cares for these men. When the decision is made to go after McCoy, Gem understands and hands the devices to Kirk and Spock, eager to help the doctor. The Vians have left them the device, hoping they will escape and leave McCoy in their grasp. The Vians must realize, though, that they will not leave; after all, it was because of their loyalty to each other that the three were brought there in the first place. Thus, the aliens are not surprised to see Kirk and Spock show up at the site of the scientific "experiments."

McCoy *will* die if Gem does not help him. Spock makes this diagnosis, and McCoy tells him, "You've got a good bedside manner, Spock." Again we see the tenderness and friendship between them. The Vians want to preserve the accuracy of their experiment by keeping Kirk and Spock out: "You must not interfere." The Vians use a force field which feeds on emotion. Gem starts to save McCoy, then grows afraid: "She's saving herself—she does not yet have the instinct to save her people." Gem seems to have some understanding of what is going on; still, she must not understand English, because the Vians openly explain their purpose in front of her: "We must wait to see if her instinct for self-sacrifice has become stronger than her instinct for self-preservation." Here, there is another tremor: "Time is short."

This lack of time, perhaps, is what induces the Vians to listen to Kirk's plea. Kirk and Spock grow angry with the Vians, though they now understand the purpose behind the torture. "You don't understand what it is to live," Kirk says. "You've lost the capacity to feel the emotions you brought Gem here to experience." Kirk is expressing our frustration at the cruelty and heartlessness of the Vians, and we are refreshed by his outburst after his prolonged helplessness. Kirk is right, of course, but what he doesn't see is that by kidnapping the three to be Gem's teachers, the Vians have admitted their weakness. Above all, the Vians are pitiful. How sad to realize what traits are "truest and best in beings . . . the qualities that make a civilization worthy to survive," and to also realize that your own race has lost those traits forever.

The Vians had planned to insist that Gem actually give up her life for McCoy (this is why they felt they had to injure McCoy so severely). After hearing Kirk, though, and perhaps because time is running out, they agree to accept Gem's offer of help as proof of her worth. The Vians, perhaps a bit ashamed, show they are not entirely dead by saving McCoy (the aliens have also learned something from the three). They carry Gem off, upward and away from us, as if to Heaven. (This is a very nice effect.) The Vians were rabidly completist in their concepts of psychological conditioning, but they were trying to make the best of a difficult situation. It wouldn't be surprising if Kirk later on felt a bit guilty about berating those pathetic creatures.

Most of "The Empath" occurs on or inside the planet (there is little of the cutting back to the *Enterprise* which usually punctuates episodes in which Kirk and company are trapped on a planet). Two basic sets are used for most of the show: the cross-like platform on which Gem heals Kirk, and the grouping of strange scientific equipment. This latter contains the body cylinders and the torture equipment, and McCoy's rectangular bed.

In many episodes of Star Trek, what seems real turns out to be illusory; in "The Empath," what seems illusory is real. The show's sets are Expressionistic, meaning they are warped and disorienting, like something out of a dream or, more exactly, a nightmare. The harsh black-and-white contrasts, very strange for the color-drenched Star Trek, bring to mind such German silent horror films as *The Cabinet of Dr. Caligari* (often called the only *truly* Expressionistic film).

In these films, shapes were used to express emotions, and realism was eschewed in favor of imbuing objects with emotional power. The emotion was often terror. Actually, Expressionism has had more of an influence on theater than film, but many movies and TV shows have had Expressionistic elements. *Night Gallery* experimented with the form, and *The Outer Limits* often used Expressionistic techniques. The classic *Outer Limits* episode entitled "Nightmare" is played out on a dark, bare stage, as is "The Empath."

"The Empath" uses several Expressionistic devices. For example, the knife-like shapes painted on the floor, the use of diagonals and triangles, and leaning shapes all serve to express a mood. Equally disorienting are the incongruous scientific equipment, some of which look more like sculpture, and the odd "ribs" (possibly appropriated from the briefing room set) which the crew walk through. Since we are inside an alien planet, we cannot actually call these sets non-realistic (who knows what such a place would really look like?), but they are Expressionistic in that they create a feeling of unease, apprehension, and fear.

The costuming is also very effective. Gem wears a bluish, diaphanous dress with jewels embroidered into it. The dress is made of gossamer, a sheer, soft fabric, and thus reflects Gem's nature. She wore a body stocking under the dress. Gem's attire contrasts with the tightness of the Starfleet uniforms. The Vians wear robes of a shiny, glittering material which suggests insulating fabric. They also wear gloves; their clothes reflect the coldness and numbness of the Vians themselves. The music and direction, by George Duning and John Erman, respectively, are also excellent.

It is an understatement to say that "The Empath" leaves unanswered questions. Alan Asherman, in his *Star Trek Compendium*, questions why the Vians didn't ask the Federation for help in saving the inhabitants of the Minaran system. But then, do aliens ever ask the Federation for help? The Gideonites, the Talosians, the Kelvans, and so on, all want to do things their own way. The real question here is, why isn't the Federation doing anything on its own to help the races facing annihilation? In "The Paradise Syndrome" and "All Our Yesterdays," the *Enterprise* is sent on such planet-saving missions. The Federation obviously knew of the impending nova long in advance; the existence of the research station proves this. So why is the Federation standing by, while the inhabitants of at least two planets are about to be wiped out?

The only possible answer to this is the Prime Directive. It states that non-spacefaring peoples, such as Gem's, are off-limits. Thus, "The Empath" presents the kind of situation which opens the Prime Directive to criticism. How can the Federation justify genocide through "non-interference"? Perhaps they simply do not feel they are ready to act as "Preservers" (unless they can do so without much chance of interference). Even the more advanced races of the Star Trek universe (i.e., Organians) try not to interfere with lesser beings. The ethic of Star Trek seems to be "Mind your own business, live and let live." Unfortunately, in this case, the ethic becomes "Live and let die."

Even if the Vians had asked the Federation for help, the Feds would have wanted it done their way. We could draw a parallel between the Vians and Kodos the Executioner. Kodos exterminated half the population of Tarsus IV to prevent the starvation of the entire colony. As Kodos said, he may have gone down as a hero had the supply ships not arrived earlier than expected. But Federation history judged him to be a mass murderer. The Vians, like Kodos, take it upon themselves to decide who is to live and who is to die. Also like Kodos, there is a certain logic and even compassion to their actions. Still, Kodos and the Vians are repulsive to us, and to the Federation.

By our standards, it is wrong to make a final judgment on the worth of an individual or race. To presume such a judgment is the height of arrogance. Such judgments are often rationalizations for evil, as was Hitler's condemnation of the Jews. And yet despite the fact that we realize no one is qualified to make such judgments, we are naturally tempted to do so. Religions get around this dilemma by invoking God; the faithful judge others, but in the name of God.

The Vians are not gods, however. Nor are their actions inspired by arrogance or malevolence. They are intelligent beings trying desperately to make the best of a bad situation. In this they are like the Talosians; misguided and desperate, but not evil. Also like the Talosians, the Vians are physical weaklings, a dying race. Saving Gem's people is their "one purpose in life." These two races, the Vians and the Talosians, form a warning of what may become of humankind. If humans lose their emotions, their ability to care about life, Star Trek proposes, they will decay into monstrous, pathetic creatures.

In "The Empath," Star Trek, as it often does, stresses the value of emotions. One could have no better teachers of this value than Kirk, Spock, and McCoy, because the nature of their relationship causes them to constantly examine emotion and logic. This theme is well developed in "The Empath." Emotions are what ultimately save the Big Three, but they also must grapple with a force field that feeds on emotion. Here it is Spock who takes advantage of his emotional control. Logic and professionalism, as embodied by the Vians and the Federation scientists, are contrasted with emotion and innocence represented in Gem. McCoy names the empath "Gem"; Scotty later likens her to "a pearl of great price." She is a gem ("mined" from underground) because of her emotional goodness. The ending, in which Mr. Scott points out that the scientific Vians valued "good old human emotion" above all, confirms this.

Yet we simply cannot sum up the episode as a paean to emotion and compassion—at least, not before addressing some other questions. First, there is the matter of why the Vians place so much value on compassion and self-sacrifice, and whether they are justified in doing so. They seem to follow the Christian ethic that lauds self-sacrifice. Thus, McCoy, the most nearly Christian character in Star Trek (he constantly uses phrases such as "Dear God" and "What in the name of Heaven . . . ?"), is the one who is (nearly) sacrificed for Gem's people.

It has been said that the mark of a civilized person is that he or she is able to place the feelings of another above his or her own. On the other hand, to sacrifice one's self for another could also be seen as a neurosis or a weakness. McCoy's line "Maybe she doesn't know [him] well enough to give up her life for him" is at the crux of this issue. Should she have to know him at all? Should she give up her life no matter how well she knows him? It is ultimately up to the individual to decide whether a tendency towards self-sacrifice is an acceptable proof for a being's worth.

The final unanswered question hanging over the

episode is, What are we to make of the Vians? Are they villainous or heroic? The Federation would not have gone along with the Vians' methods, but faced with an identical situation, could they have found a better way? If in "All Our Yesterdays," the *Enterprise* had found the inhabitants of Sarpeidon still in the path of the nova, what could they have done to help them? We have no way of answering these questions. Indeed, the crew members themselves seem reticent to pass judgment on the Vians. The final scene of "The Empath" seems unfinished, as if Kirk, Spock, and McCoy don't know quite what to make of the Vians, either.

We must take into account the real nature of the Vians' experiment. What they are doing in "The Empath" is psychologically conditioning Gem toward a certain type of behavior. They say that her compassion for another is "an instinct new to the essence of her being." This raises profound questions. Is it really possible to create such an instinct, especially in such a short period of time? Or are the Vians merely drawing out some latent instinct in Gem for compassion? It does seem highly unlikely that Gem's people would develop empathic abilities without having the emotions that would dictate their use. Why evolve into a race of empaths if there was no use for such a trait?

If Gem's self-sacrifice is truly an instinct new to her species, then we must question the worth of a race of beings who are so psychologically malleable. If Gem is so easily taught a trait we think of as good, then couldn't she (and her people) be taught evil just as readily? Gem experiences a form of social conditioning; her learning is imitative. There are no punishments or rewards involved (at least, not that she knows of). Thus, we observe a being who has acquired a new personality trait, a new pattern of behavior, simply by being shown this behavior pattern by other beings in a controlled environment. Should we judge a race of beings superior, whose identity and priorities are so changeable?

Ultimately the episode is a morality play which does not adhere to strict logic. What we know of Gem's race doesn't really make sense, and we cannot take her progression literally. Though it seems that she has been brainwashed into a false sense of morality, we obviously are not meant to perceive it that way. The Vians' method for judging Gem's race is questionable both in terms of its cruelty and its reliability. However, these logical gaps, which are only apparent after persistent study of the episode, do not hurt "The Empath." The show does not depend on literal interpretation for its effect—the Vians and Gem are primarily symbolic.

In a sense, the artificiality of the sets of "The Empath" is a kind of admission that the story is chiefly symbolic. The sets do not seem real, so we are not thinking realistically while we watch the story. "The Empath" makes use of a somewhat contrived situation to celebrate the timeless and profound beauty of the Kirk/Spock/McCoy relationship, allowing us to admire and study it. The Vians serve as representations of beings who have starved themselves of such feelings and have subsequently devolved into a pathetic, wretched state. (There is also the Christian symbolism, as several characters face death to give Gem's people a chance at life—Kirk especially is linked to crucifixion imagery.)

The importance of "The Empath" resides in its creativity and originality, and the obvious depth of feeling that inspired it. This inspiration, I think, is an appreciation of the Kirk/Spock/McCoy relationship. The episode is designed to highlight their interdependency against a dark background, as it were. In "The Empath," we delve into the underground as into the subconscious to witness a dream drama which displays the Kirk/Spock/McCoy triad in action. We see that the relationship not only improves each of the three, but also enables them to teach others—Gem, the Vians, and the audience—how to improve themselves. "The Empath" appraises the relationship of Kirk, Spock, and McCoy and concludes that it is truly a "gem," a "pearl of great price."